HAUNTED WATERS

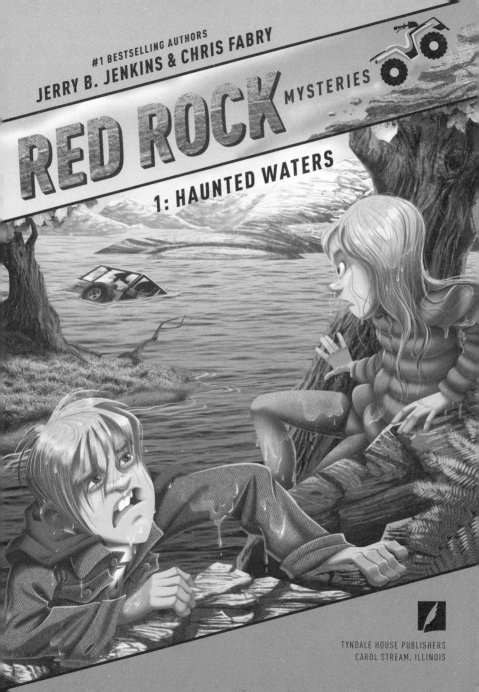

#1 BESTSELLING AUTHORS

JERRY B. JENKINS & CHRIS FABRY

RED ROCK MYSTERIES

1: HAUNTED WATERS

TYNDALE HOUSE PUBLISHERS
CAROL STREAM, ILLINOIS

Thanks to the sets of twins who consulted with us on this series,
especially Alex and Angela Wood.

Visit Tyndale's website for kids at tyndale.com/kids.

TYNDALE and Tyndale's quill logo are registered trademarks of Tyndale House Publishers.

Haunted Waters

Designed by Julie Chen

Edited by Lorie Popp

Published in association with Alive Literary Agency, Inc., www.aliveliterary.com.

Haunted Waters is a work of fiction. Where real people, events, establishments, organizations, or locales appear, they are used fictitiously. All other elements of the novel are drawn from the authors' imaginations.

For manufacturing information regarding this product, please call 1-800-323-9400.

For information about special discounts for bulk purchases, please contact Tyndale House Publishers at csresponse@tyndale.com, or call 1-800-323-9400.

ISBN 978-1-4964-4938-2

Printed in the United States of America

26 25 24 23 22 21
7   6   5   4   3   2

This book is for Kristen Rebecca Fabry.

"I am HAUNTED by WATERS."

NORMAN MACLEAN,
A River Runs Through It

"COURAGE is FEAR that has said its PRAYERS."

DOROTHY BERNARD

He didn't want to kill them. He just wanted the evidence back. If they made it to the police with the picture, he was dead. Back in jail.

If only those annoying kids hadn't forced this. Twins. A boy and a girl. And their little brother and dad. Now they would all have to pay.

He could see the fright in the kids' eyes when he pulled beside their Land Cruiser. The boy held a cell phone to his ear.

He rammed his vehicle into theirs and sent them swerving. The dad got the Cruiser under control and sped up.

He matched their speed and pulled beside them again as they

approached a lake. This was it. He would take care of the problem right here. He turned and forced them off the road.

The Land Cruiser hit a patch of snowy grass. Taillights flashed, but it was too late. The SUV flew into the air and plunged into the lake. Water engulfed the vehicle and it slowly rolled to one side like a sunning sea lion, then sank.

He slowed to watch frigid bubbles rise. No one could survive this. Some mother would cry tonight.

He clicked his radio as he drove away. "The situation's under control."

PART 1

CHAPTER 1

ASHLEY

I didn't want to move to Colorado. I didn't want my dad to die or my mom to ever get married again either. And I sure didn't want her to get religious all of a sudden. But all those things happened to my brother and me, so I guess you'll just have to get used to it like we did.

My name is Ashley Timberline, and my younger brother (by 57 seconds—but he's still younger) is Bryce. We're almost 14, if 217 days is almost. Our last name used to be Bishop, but our new dad adopted us, so now we've got his name. Good thing Mom didn't name me Fern or Tabby. Imagine that with my new last name. Mom said we didn't *have* to take the new name, but I would have felt bad hurting our stepfather's feelings.

My youngest brother, Dylan, who is four, was born before our real dad died. He's a pain, but he's a lot cuter than Bryce, and I can get him to do stuff just by offering him a couple of Smarties.

We also got a big sister thrown in with our new dad. Leigh's 16 and learning to drive. She has a boyfriend named Randy, but Bryce and I call him The Creep. He's actually kind of cute, with hair he never combs and big muscles. But we give her a hard time about him anyway.

Randy played on the varsity football team in the fall and now varsity baseball this spring. He's always getting his name in the paper, and once there was a picture of him making a big tackle. I wrote "The Creep takes down his opponent" underneath it, and Leigh got mad. Not as mad as the time Bryce dipped her hairbrush in the fish tank, but mad enough to tell her dad. He came in and sat on my bed and grinned for about five minutes, then left.

The hardest thing we've ever done is move from Illinois. When we drove away from our little house, it seemed like we left every friend we'd ever had. The new people were already moving in, which was sad. We'd written our names in the cement by the driveway. Half of Dylan's car collection is still buried in the backyard. The cheap swing set my mom bought at a garage sale is still under that big, leafy tree.

My friend Carolyn said she was jealous of me getting to move out west, making a new start. I would have traded places with her in a second. There were enough new things going on without having to move 1,000 miles. Mom said "the Lord" was guiding her even back then before she knew him. But whoever the Lord was, he wasn't doing anything but making me cry myself to sleep in the backseat of our Ford Taurus Wagon.

I stopped sobbing when we hit the Illinois/Iowa state line and snorted myself to sleep. I woke up long enough to eat in Missouri, then cried again after dessert—a Reese's Peanut Butter Cup Blizzard. Bryce didn't sleep at all and said I didn't miss much on the drive, except a guy hitchhiking near Salina, Kansas. Bryce said the guy had a beard longer than we were tall and he was sitting by a dead deer with a banjo. (The guy had the banjo, not the deer.)

When we got to Colorado, the first thing Dylan did was throw up. That made me think things were going to be really yucky here, but Mom said it was only the altitude—living so far above sea level where the air is thinner. Less oxygen for some reason. If you ever come here, you might throw up too.

A year later Mom fell in love with The Cowboy, as we called Sam back then. They were married, and we moved to his place. Then Mom became a Christian, and not because of our new dad, because he wasn't—and isn't—one. Bryce and I thought Mom was just going through a holy phase, but when it stuck, we got interested too. Finally, Bryce and I became Christians.

I thought I'd always been one, but that's another story.

CHAPTER 2

BRYCE

My cell phone vibrated with only a few minutes left in my last-period class. I pulled it out and hid it under my desk, because you're not supposed to use cell phones during class. I looked at my sister Ashley a few rows from me. We have first and last periods together—band and English.

The screen on the front read "Bryce's Phone," showed the time as 2:14, and had a little envelope telling me I had a text message. I coughed as I punched the Read button so the teacher wouldn't hear the beep, then scrolled through the message.

Surprise for you and Ashley. Come home as fast as you can. Also, move snow shovel from porch. Somebody'll get hurt.

See you soon.

The message was from Sam, my new father. Ashley and I haven't felt right about calling him Dad since our real one died. Sam said if we never call him Dad, it would be okay, but if we wanted to it was all right too.

Those last six minutes dragged so slowly I could hardly stand it. Giving a kid English during last period ought to be a crime, punishable by torture if you have gym right before it.

Mrs. Ferguson went on and on about how important next week was for us. "As you know, you have the day off tomorrow and then the CATs begin Monday. Make sure you take advantage of the long weekend."

We'd been hearing about the Colorado Aptitude Tests for a whole year, since the last time we had taken them, so this was not news.

"Get plenty of sleep Sunday night," she continued. "Try not to do anything that would sap your energy. We want you all bright-eyed Monday."

Ashley rolled her eyes at me.

I held up the little beanie cat that had been passed around the room to motivate us and grabbed it around the neck.

Ashley looked like she was fighting a smile.

I glanced at the clock again. I think when the sun gets high in the sky, it loses some kind of gravity pull and everything slows down. Whatever, the seconds t-i-c-k-e-d by in agony until the bell finally rang. I tossed the cat to Mrs. Ferguson, and it landed on her desk next to her big, yellow thesaurus.

"Have a nice weekend, Bryce," she purred.

"You too, Mrs. Ferguson."

Ashley followed as I raced into the halls of Red Rock Middle School. I threw my books in my locker. CATs kept teachers from giving us homework—that's about the only good thing about them. I slammed my locker and saw Aaron Heckler at the end of the hall.

CHAPTER 3

ASHLEY

Bryce froze when Boo Heckler called his name. The big eighth grader stood at the end of the hall under one of the stuffed cats the school had hung there for the assembly earlier in the week. The drama teacher had even dressed up in one of the costumes from the musical *Cats* for it.

Everyone calls Aaron Heckler Boo because that's what he yells at every sporting event. Every referee, umpire, or official hears his boo waft over fields and through gymnasiums. He boos when the referees are introduced. He boos when someone calls a time-out. We heard he even booed at a spelling bee his first year of middle school.

"Hey, Timberline!" Boo boomed through the hall.

To say Boo is scary is like saying the Grand Canyon is deep or Mount Everest is tall. He's bigger than most of the teachers and has long, apelike arms that dangle like tree limbs. His hair always hangs in his face, except for once or twice a year when he gets it cut. He has yellow fingertips, and Bryce says that's because he smokes. His teeth look like a multicolored Popsicle—green at the top, yellow in the middle, and orange at the bottom.

Several boys usually hang around with Boo, probably because they're afraid of him too. I couldn't imagine what Bryce had done to flash on Boo's radar screen.

"Saw you and your sister ride up on those four-wheelers today," he hollered.

"Great," Bryce muttered.

"Let's get out of here," I whispered.

"Hey, sis," Boo called, walking toward us.

Kids on the way to their buses hung around as long as they could. I guess to see what would happen. A couple of my friends gritted their teeth and stared at me. It was like watching a train wreck. You didn't want to see what was about to happen, but you couldn't turn away either.

"You two splashed mud on my friend," Boo continued, nodding at someone behind him, his big feet clomping toward us. "We're lookin' for payback."

"I don't remember passing anyone this morning," I said.

A boy about half Boo's size stepped from behind him with a few mud splatters on his shirt and pants. Some of them looked fresh, which was strange if we'd splashed him hours before. I started to say something, but Bryce put a hand in the air and said, "I-I'm sorry your c-c-clothes got mud on them. We ride through the pasture, so I'm not sure how we could have—"

"You callin' my friend a liar?" Boo said, stepping closer. He had a small scar above his right cheek, and his socks stuck through holes in the sides of his sneakers. If he wasn't so mean, I would have felt sorry for him.

"It was him and his sister," the smaller boy said, pointing.

Bryce, looking pale, folded his arms. He stutters sometimes, especially when he's nervous, but it doesn't seem to bother him. "W-what do you want me to d-do about it?"

I was ticked that Bryce wouldn't let me talk, but I figured he was protecting me. And that made me madder.

I turned and walked away, hoping to find a teacher.

CHAPTER 4

BRYCE

I was glad when Ashley left. Nobody wants his sister to watch him get beat up. I didn't want her to see me cry or bleed.

The longer I faced Boo, the drier my throat got. It was hard to breathe, and I could feel my heart thumping.

I'd never been in a fight. I'd been in shoving and shouting matches where nobody really gets hurt, but I'd never been in a ball-your-hand-into-a-fist-and-start-swinging kind of thing. This was quickly turning into a get-smashed-like-a-bug fight.

I kept thinking of Jesus saying to turn the other cheek. But turning the other cheek to this guy could mean a short life or at least plastic surgery. Did Jesus ever get into a fight when he was a kid? I wished Boo was a money changer so I could turn over his tables.

"Hit him, Bryce!" somebody shouted. It was my friend Duncan Swift. He'd been in more fights than Mike Tyson and always had a few bruises.

"L-look, I-I-I don't want to fight you," I said.

Boo and the other kid laughed. Boo said, "Did you hear that? Sounds like h-h-he can't figure out whether he's a b-b-boy or a g-g-girl. Your sister's more of a man than you are."

A few people ran for their buses, but there was still a crowd. I locked eyes with Boo and tried to stare him down.

"Let us take your four-wheelers home for the weekend," Boo said, steely eyed. "We'll bring 'em back Monday and call it even."

Sam had told us not to let anybody, no matter how trustworthy, ride our ATVs. I was catching on to Boo's game. They'd faked the mud splatters to get our bikes.

"No way," I said. "My dad won't let—"

Boo lurched forward and jabbed his finger hard into my shoulder. "Your dad won't know unless you tell him."

I heard a commotion down the hall. Ashley ran toward us with Mr. Micelli, our science teacher.

Boo gripped my shoulder and turned me around. "We're gonna get those four-wheelers. You don't let us ride them and you'll be sorry."

"What's going on?" Mr. Micelli said.

Boo turned and walked away.

Mr. Micelli put a hand on my back. He didn't have to say anything. He had to know I was scared.

"You should have hit him, Timberline," Duncan said, grabbing his backpack and leaving. "Bigger they are, the harder they fall."

More likely, the harder I'll fall.

I tried to think of something snappy to say to get everybody to laugh, but my bottom lip twitched, and everything I thought of was kind of mean.

"Come on," Ashley said, taking my backpack.

CHAPTER 5

ASHLEY

My ATV, the Ashleymobile, is one of the best things about moving to Colorado. My friends back home can't believe I actually get to ride it to school, except when it's raining really hard. Kids under 16 shouldn't ride them, but Mom and Sam say we're pretty responsible. Sometimes Mom sends us to the grocery store for milk or bread, and we've found a way there without going on too many streets. We even drive to the gas station and fill up by ourselves.

I reached Mrs. Watson's barn first, strapped on my helmet, and fastened my backpack to the rear carrier. We always park our ATVs a few blocks from the school at Mrs. Watson's. She knows our stepfather, and Bryce mows her yard. She says she loves having us around.

Bryce's eyes were puffy and red. You can tell a lot about people just by looking at their eyes, especially when they won't look at you.

Mrs. Watson waved and offered us a snack, but Bryce yelled that Sam wanted us home for something. After we started the four-wheelers, I glanced across the road and punched Bryce's shoulder. On the hill above the school stood Boo and his muddy little friend.

Bryce took off up Mrs. Watson's driveway toward the open pasture, and I followed.

Boo shouted something and waved, and I hoped Mrs. Watson didn't have her hearing aid in.

CHAPTER 6

BRYCE

I was never so happy to get home in my life. Mom stood by the front door with a smile. She hugged me, then nodded at the snow shovel by the front porch. "How was your day, Bryce?"

I shrugged.

"He almost got beat up," Ashley said.

"I did not." I gave Ashley a dagger stare.

"How's your book coming, Mom?" Ashley said.

"I'm getting there."

My mom's a writer and works while we're at school and when she's not driving Dylan to somebody's house to play or picking him up from preschool. She writes novels under the name Virginia Caldwell, which I think is cool. Lots of people read the books but have no idea she's the one who writes them.

"Where's Sam?" I said.

"In his office."

I sprinted out back to the old barn with Ashley at my heels. It had been built something like a hundred years ago, and the bottom level looks like a movie set from one of those old Westerns you see on Nickelodeon. We don't have any horses, but old saddles still hang on the walls and a few bales of hay are scattered around.

A staircase covered in carpet leads up the wall, and there are pictures of famous people who have ridden in Sam's planes. He's been the pilot for movie stars, athletes, authors, and politicians. They pay him, and that's how he makes money. Most of the pictures are signed by these people and say things like, "Thanks, Sam, you're the best" and "Great flight, you're the best." Some of the movie stars have asked him to work for them full time, but Sam says he likes his freedom.

I burst into the office without knocking to find him on the phone with his feet up on his desk. The office is half the size of the entire stable, with a countertop that runs around the walls. There are filing cabinets and drawers everywhere, a big bookcase, a ceiling fan, and little helicopters and planes here and there. From the front window you can see our house, the red rock formation in the distance, and due south, the snowy cap of Pikes Peak.

On the other side of the office is a bathroom with a shower and an exercise room. When we moved in, Sam bought a little TV with some video games so Ashley and I could play.

Sam put a finger to his lips and kept talking. He has a deep, growly voice, something between a bear and a football announcer, and he talks slowly. "Okay, that sounds good. What time do you need to be in Aspen?"

Ashley sat in a huge leather chair and put her feet up like she owned the place. The leather creaked as she tilted back and smiled. I almost forgot Boo Heckler.

CHAPTER 7

ASHLEY

Sam hung up and faced Bryce and me. "How would you two like to go on a little trip with me?"

"To Aspen?" I said.

"No, that's Monday. I saw this in the paper today and thought you and Bryce might like a little Colorado educational experience. How would you like to see a vug?"

"A what?" I said.

He handed me a clipping from the local paper, the *Red Rock Post*, and Bryce knelt beside me. We read the headline out loud: "'Historic Vug On Display in Gold Town.'"

Bryce hit my arm and said, "Slug-vug, no slug backs."
It was so corny I had to laugh.

A re-creation of a hidden golden chamber discovered in the
early 1900s will be on display this weekend along with a rare
gold nugget.

One of the most impressive exhibits in the newly created
Gold Town shows tourists what miners saw when they blasted
into a hollow area and discovered gold and crystals sparkling
on the walls. Also on display will be a priceless gold nugget in
its original form.

"You know how much Dylan talks about those old mines," Sam
said. "Thought I'd take him along too."

"What about Mom?" I said.

"She's trying to complete her book. I told her she could have a
weekend alone—at least mostly alone. Leigh's finishing her driving
course."

Bryce shrugged. "I have a basketball game Saturday."

"I've already talked with your coach," Sam said, then looked at
me. "And Mom says there's no dance lesson until next week."

Bryce frowned. "I don't know if I want to go all that way just to
look at a hole and a nugget."

"That's just part of the trip," Sam said. "A businessman I flew
a couple of weeks ago offered us his cabin this weekend. The vug
display is close. Plus, there's hiking, skiing, and tubing if the weather
cooperates."

"Is the cabin 'rustic'?" I said. "Because every time I've been in a
cabin somebody said was 'rustic,' I've sneezed my head off from all
the dust."

"You've been to one cabin in your life," Bryce said.

Sam chuckled. "I've never been to this place, but my friend said it has a hot tub, satellite TV—the works. Doesn't sound rustic, and I don't think you'll have to worry about dust."

"Do we have to babysit?" I said.

"No, I'll take care of Dylan. You two can wander off on your own."

Bryce glanced at me with wide eyes. I could tell he was looking for any excuse to get away from Red Rock and the shadow of Boo Heckler.

To be honest, skiing, tubing, and hiking are nice, but I like being inside, curling up with a good book or watching a movie. But since coming to Colorado I've developed more of a taste for adventure.

"Let's do it," I said.

CHAPTER 8

BRYCE

"Can you pass the potatoes, Bryce?" Leigh said.

I handed her the basket of wedges, and she threw a few on her plate and squirted some ketchup. "Nothing like a home-cooked meal," she said with a smirk.

Sam raised his eyebrows at her, but she kept her head down.

"Sorry about the takeout," Mom said. "I've been trying to finish this book."

"I like the chicken," Dylan said, pulling the skin from a piece and stuffing it in his mouth. Dylan is a world champion chicken-skin eater. I don't think he's eaten a piece of meat in his life, but he eats the skin like it's candy.

A horn honked, and Leigh stood and looked in a mirror. She has long, brown hair and a nice smile like her real mom. I've seen the picture she keeps in her bedroom. It's been tough for her to get used to having the four of us in her territory. And with Mom becoming a Christian and Leigh and her dad not, well, it's made for interesting conversations.

"Is that The Creep?" I whispered to Ashley, craning my neck to see out the window.

"Stop calling him that," Leigh said.

"Oh, he doesn't mean it in a bad way," Ashley said. "We think he's a nice creep."

Dylan snatched another chicken skin and ran toward the door, crumbs scattering on the carpet. "The Creep!" he yelled.

"Dad!" Leigh said, dragging a brush through her hair.

Mom collared Dylan and brought him back to the table, clearing her throat and glaring at Ashley and me.

"Sorry," Ashley said.

"Why don't you ask Randy to come in and have some chicken?" Sam said.

"No way," Leigh said. "He's helping me practice parallel parking."

Sam followed her outside and returned a few minutes later with Randy.

Leigh bit her lip and plopped into a chair while Mom grabbed another plate.

"So, how's baseball season?" I said.

"Pretty good," Randy said, taking a bite. "This is excellent chicken, Mrs. Timberline."

"Thank the colonel," Leigh said.

Sam gave Leigh another look, and she passed the gravy.

"Leigh tells me you and your sister get to drive those four-wheelers to school. Pretty cool."

"Yeah, we think so. How's Leigh's driving?"

He took a biscuit. "I'm going to have her parking on a postage stamp. She's doing great."

Dylan stared at Randy's cutoff shirt and his underarm. I tried to get Dylan's attention, but he kept looking. Finally he said, "You have hair under there."

"Okay, time to go," Leigh said.

Randy laughed, took the chicken with him, and thanked Mom again.

Sam looked at Ashley and me like he wanted to say something. I felt bad about calling Randy names.

Dylan snagged another chicken skin and smiled. "Dessert."

CHAPTER 9

ASHLEY

While Bryce watched a hockey game with Sam, Mom drove me to my friend Hayley's house. I've known Hayley since starting at Red Rock Middle School. She and her family have visited our church, Mountain View Chapel, but they haven't come for a while. I'm pretty sure Hayley's not a Christian.

I expected Mom to lecture me about Leigh and Randy, but she didn't say a word, which was even more upsetting. I'd rather be yelled at when I deserve it than get the silent treatment. Plus, if you're yelled at, you can say you're sorry, cry, and get some sympathy.

I told Mom I'd call when we were through with our social studies project (which was basically an excuse for us to get together, because it wasn't due until a week from Monday). I waved as she drove away, but she didn't look back.

Hayley met me at the door, and we went to her kitchen. The house was quiet. She said her parents had gone out to dinner, which was okay, but I had told Mom they would be here.

"I want to watch the rest of a movie," Hayley said. "Come on. There's only about 15 minutes left."

I thought about calling Mom, because that was our agreement. If I wanted to watch something I'd never seen, I needed to check in. But Hayley got two cans of Coke from the refrigerator and headed for the living room so fast I didn't have time to think.

"It's a love story," Hayley said. "Don't you just love love stories?"

"Sure."

But what came on the TV wasn't what I expected. The language was worse than at the construction site Bryce and I used to walk past in Chicago. Hayley didn't seem to mind, and though I thought about leaving the room, I felt glued to my chair, embarrassed.

The language got worse, and then the shooting started. Blood flew everywhere. I almost couldn't look, but Hayley just stared.

A few minutes later a car pulled up. Hayley turned the TV off and hurried to the kitchen. It was her older sister.

I felt bad because I hadn't stopped watching the movie. I was mixed up and didn't know what to do.

When Hayley's sister went upstairs, Hayley asked if I wanted to watch the rest of the movie.

"Nah. I'd rather work on the project."

CHAPTER 10

BRYCE

I could tell Ashley was upset when she came home, but I didn't know why. I figured it was because Mom had yelled at her about The Creep thing. Sam and I talked a little about it during the Avalanche game, but he didn't get on me too much. He just said I should lay off Leigh for a while about Randy, and I said I would.

There was a break in the game when one player hit the Avs center with his stick and knocked him down. There was a lot of blood, and the announcers couldn't believe the officials hadn't called a penalty. I stared at the player who had hit him and saw Boo's face. I had to close my eyes.

I asked Sam if he thought that last play was a penalty.

Sam sat up straight as a news report flashed on the screen—something about a terrorist capture in France. "Hang on a minute," he said. "I want to hear this."

Usually he listens pretty well. You know how grown-ups can pretend they're listening when they're really not, and they look right through you, then ask you to repeat what you've just said? Sam hadn't done that with me much, but this time he was so focused on the TV that I went to make some popcorn.

I walked upstairs while it popped and knocked on Ashley's door. She was on her bed writing in her diary, her scented candle burning on her nightstand. Every time she writes in her diary she has to light the candle. She says it gives her inspiration. It smells like pumpkins and cinnamon and makes me want to go on a hayride.

She didn't look up, which was my signal to go back downstairs and leave her alone. I let Pippin and Frodo (our two dogs) outside and grabbed the popcorn from the microwave.

PART 2

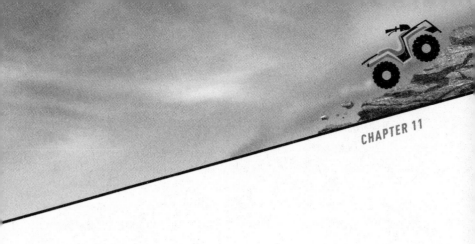

CHAPTER 11

ASHLEY

Sam woke us before daylight Friday morning, and we hurried to get ready. Bryce carried both of our backpacks while I helped Dylan find his water bottle and stuffed raccoon. We said good-bye to Pippin and Frodo.

Mom caught us at the door and kissed us all. She had come in my room the night before while I was writing in my journal and asked if I wanted to talk, but I said I didn't. Now I felt guilty for not telling her about watching the movie with Hayley.

"Did you get your medicine?" she said, kissing the top of my head.

I rolled my eyes and went back to the kitchen cupboard. Since I was eight I've had to take pills to control a seizure disorder. Mom says it's not a big deal, that the doctor says I'll grow out of it, but sometimes it feels like I'm getting worse. I stuffed the two bottles in my jacket pocket and raced to the Land Cruiser.

"Have a good time," Mom called from the door.

She stood there as we pulled away, waving and smiling. I knew exactly what she'd do after she closed the door. She'd make a pot of coffee and head upstairs to the office Sam had built for her. Like his, it looks out on the mountains, but the inside is decorated with pictures of our family, famous writers, and our dogs. She also has knick-knacks, candles, and quotes like, "Nothing—unless it is difficult—is worthwhile" and "The wastepaper basket is the writer's best friend."

When the sun comes up, she'll be looking out at Pikes Peak, typing away. She says writing does something for her that nothing else does, but I'm not sure what. Maybe it puts her into a different world, and she likes that because her own world has been pretty painful.

Bryce and I fought for the front seat. Sam finally said Bryce could have it on the way there and I could have it on the way back. I pouted and tried to sleep beside Dylan's car seat as we rumbled south on I-25. The interstate cuts a path past the Front Range of mountains between Denver and Colorado Springs. We passed the Air Force Academy and its huge football stadium. I noticed the exit for Focus on the Family and peered into the darkness to see if I could make out Whit's End and the giant green slide that runs down one side of the building. I noticed a lump by the road, and when we got closer, I saw it was a huge animal.

"That's a bull elk," Sam said. "Wouldn't want to see the car that hit the thing."

I wondered if the elk's family would miss him as much as we missed our dad.

Soon we were heading west on Route 24 toward the mountains, and I couldn't keep my eyes open.

When I woke up, we were parked in front of a grocery store. "Where are we?" I said.

"Woodland Park," Sam said. "This is the last store we'll see for a while. Let's get some supplies and keep going. I want to hit the pass before the sun comes up."

I didn't know what he was talking about but followed him inside.

He put Dylan in a shopping cart shaped like a car and pushed another one in front of Bryce and me. "Dylan and I will get everything for sandwiches and burgers," he said. "You two get the good stuff."

"What do you mean?" Bryce said.

Sam leaned close and smiled. "Chips, soda, candy, popcorn—all the stuff your mom wouldn't like. You have 10 minutes."

Bryce and I took off. Mom fixes healthy foods and snacks, but she's not against an occasional trip to McDonald's. Somehow, I thought Sam and she had planned this—a weekend of bonding with the stepdad—but right now I didn't care.

We zipped down the chip aisle, picking out sour cream and onion, barbecue, and thick chips for dipping. Bryce grabbed some huge pretzels, and I found a tin of cashews I thought Sam would like.

In 10 minutes we had the cart full of food. It would probably take us a year to eat it all.

CHAPTER 12

BRYCE

I helped Sam load our food in the SUV while Ashley buckled Dylan into his car seat. The store had been fun, except that the guy who bagged our stuff looked like Boo Heckler's muddy little friend. I couldn't help but think of school Monday. If Boo kept pressuring Ashley and me to loan him our ATVs, we'd have to stop driving them. And if his threats were real, I was in trouble. I didn't see any way out except for wearing a catcher's mask and taking the bus to school.

As Sam drove up an incline, the sun glinted in the side mirror. The clouds turned orange-gold, and a line of yellow light sparkling against the horizon totally took my mind off Boo.

"What is this place?" Ashley said, leaning forward from the backseat.

"Wilkerson Pass," Sam said. "Most incredible scene in the whole state if you ask me."

"What's so special about it?" I said.

Sam reached the top of the hill and slowed. "Take a look."

My jaw dropped. The whole world seemed to open up. The road stretched all the way to the mountains for what seemed like 100 miles. There were a few farmhouses here and there, but it was mostly open range. A hawk flew overhead, looking for prey.

"Amazing," Ashley whispered.

"It's the Great Valley!" Dylan said, obviously remembering one of his *Land Before Time* videos.

Sam chuckled. "And most of it has stayed the same for hundreds of years. What you're seeing right now is what the Native Americans and the pioneers saw as they rode through here."

A few stars were left over from the night, and the moon was still full over the whole area. A couple of miles farther we wound our way down the mountain and saw buffalo near a stream. Sam stopped and we got out to look at the huge beasts.

Suddenly the buffalo took off, stampeding across the valley. I don't know what scared them, but the sight made me dread Boo Heckler again.

CHAPTER 13

ASHLEY

This was like seeing Pikes Peak for the first time. I closed my eyes and let the scene etch itself in my memory.

We headed back to a visitors center for cookies and hot chocolate. Bryce was staring at pictures and exhibits of pioneer life, but I knew his mind was somewhere else. We got in the Land Cruiser and backtracked to some curvy roads. I thought I was going to get sick, and I was even more scared that Dylan would upchuck his fruit snacks. But Sam put down the windows, and we all took a breath of fresh air. Once I looked straight down a cliff, which made me want to roll my window back up.

I've always been afraid on bridges, scared that the car would plunge into the water and we wouldn't make it out. One time I dreamed we all got out except Dylan, who was trapped in his car seat, and I spent the rest of the night in Mom's room. I couldn't believe how glad I was to see him the next morning and give him a hug, Pop-Tarts crumbs and all.

"So, you kids have been here more than a year now," Sam said as we passed some kind of reservoir. The water was right next to the SUV so I could see swirls on top from where fish swam. A sign said Scenic Overlook Ahead.

Sam looked at me in the rearview mirror. "What do you think so far?"

I shrugged. "It's okay."

Sam frowned.

I know he wanted me to say Colorado was the best place on earth, that I was "happy as a raccoon in a cornfield," as my grandfather would say. But my real dad was dead, my mom was busy, and I just hadn't "connected" with Sam yet—which confirmed my suspicions about the weekend.

"It's cool we get to ride the ATVs to school," Bryce said.

"I like my waccoon and monkey." Dylan looked around and found his stuffed raccoon and Chunky Monkey, which was made out of a sock. Sam had bought the monkey at the grocery store.

After a few wrong turns we made it to the driveway of the cabin. Sam got out and unhooked a chain. Then we drove into the woods. Even though it was morning, it looked like night because there were so many trees. The road was muddy, and we lurched up the hill in four-wheel drive.

Bryce gasped when he saw the place. It was a big A-frame surrounded by trees, except at the back where the house overlooked a cliff. Just like earlier, it felt like you could see forever.

We made two trips to bring our backpacks and all the groceries inside. Before we could explore, Sam handed us both tiny walkie-talkies and showed us how to work them.

"How far will these reach?" Bryce said.

"A few miles, depending on the mountains."

Sam must have seen the look on my face. "I don't plan on us splitting up this weekend. This is just to be safe."

CHAPTER 14

BRYCE

The cabin was incredible. Ashley and I walked around the main floor and found the kitchen, two bedrooms, a bathroom, and a huge living room with a fireplace in the middle and windows big enough for Godzilla. There was also a loft, and Sam carried his and Dylan's stuff up there. The view out over the mountain took my breath away, and the first thing I wanted to do was draw it for Mom. Ashley took a shot with her digital camera.

Ashley claimed the best bedroom, the one with bunk beds. She said since she didn't get to ride up front, she had dibs. I threw my backpack in the next room.

Then we headed to the lower level. Not only was there a Ping-Pong table and a pool table, but there was also a real Lord of the Rings pinball machine with lights and bells and buzzers. At one end of the room a TV was hooked up to the satellite, and there were a bunch of movies in the cabinet underneath.

"Guess that's for if we get snowed in," Ashley said.

"I wouldn't mind getting snowed in here for the rest of my life," I said. "Wish we'd have brought the dogs."

On the wall by the pinball machine was a picture of a weird-looking woman. She wore a red dress and stared at the camera. Her face gave me the willies.

Ashley opened a cabinet and found a screaming-fast computer. "We can e-mail Mom my picture!"

"Let's go shoot some more."

But Sam said it was time to see Gold Town. The pictures would have to wait.

CHAPTER 15

Gavin Winkler parked the dark green rental car in the gravel at the end of the Gold Town parking lot. He lit a cigarette and flicked on the radio, skipping through music, talk shows, and news reports.

Gavin had checked out of his hotel in Denver in the wee hours, leaving his key in his room and a mountain of room-service dishes. He couldn't leave a trail here, so as inviting as it looked, he wouldn't be staying at the little bed-and-breakfast nearby. This would be a quick job. In and out. Get the goods and take off. He wanted no one to see him.

A friend had introduced Gavin to the man who had set up their little operation. The man wanted someone slick, someone clean-cut, who had never been to jail. Gavin had lied about his past. He had spent time in prison—a lot of it actually. But the man didn't need to know. Things had been stolen. People hurt.

Gavin scrunched down in his seat and watched the parking lot fill with vehicles. Mostly SUVs. Moms and dads with little kiddies who wanted to see the golden trinket and the sparkly room. The radio gave the weather: a chance of snow Saturday in the higher elevations. Perfect. He'd be out of town and on to Las Vegas before anyone knew what had happened.

He focused on the shiny trailer by the wooden building. Inside were photos and artifacts of the gold rush. People had traveled here more than 100 years ago hoping to change their lives, to get rich.

Gavin was going to do the same, only he wouldn't even have to get his hands dirty.

CHAPTER 16

ASHLEY

We made it to Gold Town that afternoon. The exhibit trailer
and General Store were packed. Sam let us out and parked in a
muddy area next to the parking lot. Bryce held Dylan's hand so he
wouldn't break away and run toward the fake mine shaft up the hill.

The black-and-gold trailer with the vug inside was parked near
a rock looming above the town. I snapped a picture, then followed
the others inside the store.

Ropes were set up to show people where to walk. Sam put Dylan
on his shoulders so he could see over people's heads.

The shop smelled musty, like Mrs. Watson's basement, and on

the walls were black-and-white pictures, mostly of bearded miners with burros. One showed a woman in a white dress on a wooden sidewalk, shielding her eyes from the sun. Another was of a man inside a mine, his face dirty. I wondered what had happened to these people. Had they spent their entire lives in Colorado or moved farther west chasing some dream? Had they stayed poor or struck gold and become rich?

Soon after we entered, the store owner began his presentation. "From the late 1850s until almost 1900, newspapers carried stories of people like you see in those pictures, poor and lonely, who came to Colorado, saw a glint of light in a stream or off a rock, and came back millionaires. Most didn't strike it rich, and the ones who did were usually the ones who set up stores and saloons. But every now and then someone found gold."

The man looked around the room. "I don't suppose any of you younger people have heard the story of Horace Tabor?"

Every middle schooler in Colorado had to have heard the story, so I was surprised that no one but Bryce raised a hand.

"Yes, young man. What happened to him?"

"Um . . . wasn't he the g-guy wh-who traded his store for a silver mine?"

"Yes, but not the whole store," the man said, pointing to a picture of a man with a large mustache. "Born in Vermont in 1830, he and his wife heard of the riches being found in Colorado, moved here, and opened a general store much like this one. One day two grizzled miners came into his business and asked him to 'grubstake' them, which meant if Tabor would supply them with picks, shovels, and food, they would give him one-third of the share of the mine. On May 15, 1878, Tabor rushed up Fryer Hill from his store after hearing the two men had hit pay dirt. The silver mine made Tabor rich."

People smiled and shook their heads.

Before the shop owner could continue, Sam said, "Tell them how the story ended."

The shop owner frowned. "He died in Denver in 1899, leaving a wife and two daughters penniless. He went from rags to riches and back to rags."

The owner then told the story of the gold nugget on display, how a poor prospector named Jedediah Maxwell, who had nearly frozen to death and had been attacked by bears, finally struck it rich in a nearby mine. He held up a glass-encased nugget that looked like it weighed a ton. "This was one of the first nuggets Jedediah discovered, and he vowed that no one would touch it. He kept it hidden, and only after his death did a friend find it in a secret compartment under his desk."

People gawked at the gold, and I wished I could hold it.

The owner went on. "A few years later, some miners were blasting about 1,200 feet down when they discovered what geologists call a vug. The room was about 23 feet long, 14 feet wide, and 36 feet high—exactly the same as you'll see inside the exhibit."

The man paused dramatically. "No one but those miners ever saw what that room looked like. Armed men guarded it day and night. No pictures were ever taken. But artists have gone over the miners' eyewitness accounts of that room, and when you're led in, you will see what they might have seen almost 100 years ago."

CHAPTER 17

BRYCE

People passed by the huge nugget on their way to the exhibit. A woman sold replicas of it, along with snacks and soda. Ashley tugged at my arm to get in line and I followed, hoping we'd get to take some fake gold home. Sam and Dylan were already way ahead of us, and Dylan pointed at a toy miner's hat with a light in it.

A well-dressed man stood behind the glass to make sure no one tried to touch the nugget.

"I'll bet you have that thing insured," a tourist said.

"For 50 million, sir," the owner said. A muscular guard stood behind him.

It wasn't that exciting, seeing some hunk of gold a dead guy had hidden. Dylan wriggled down and ran from the store, his miner's hat shifting on his head and Sam hurrying after him. A stranger at the doorway looked straight at Ashley and me. He walked to the front and talked with the store owner.

We were only three people away from the nugget now. I pointed at Ashley's camera, but she shook her head. When she turned to look at some fake rocks on the counter, I grabbed the camera and shot a picture of the nugget. As soon as the flash went off, the well-dressed man was next to me.

"Pictures aren't allowed," he said, his mouth tight.

I couldn't see any sign that said No Pictures Allowed. My face got hot, and I knew my cheeks were red. I hate when that happens. It felt like everybody was staring at me, and I was nervous. The camera slipped and bonked on the floor. The memory stick snapped out and clattered away.

"Nice work, Captain Clumso," Ashley whispered.

I scooped up the camera and handed it to Ashley. She inspected it and frowned, but I could tell it still worked.

The shop owner was next to me now. "I'll have to ask for the film from that camera."

"I-I'm sorry," I said. "I didn't see a sign."

"Whose children are these?" the store owner said, ignoring me. He said it like we were a couple of muddy dogs who had run over his white carpet.

"They're mine," Sam said from behind us. He was carrying Dylan, and I was glad he was back. He walked toward us as the crowd parted. "I'm sure this was an innocent mistake."

The owner frowned. "I would ask you to control your children."

Sam stared at the man with a look I hadn't seen before, like a tiger that's been in a cage too long.

"It's digital," Ashley said. "I can delete the picture."

The owner seized the camera and seemed to know how to work it. He went through every picture Ashley had shot—the ones of the front of the cabin, the view from the window, even one of me sleeping with my Cubs blanket, which I didn't know she had taken.

The man studied a photo—a bit too long, I thought—then hit the Delete button. Then he deleted the entire set of pictures she had taken. "Just to be sure," he said, handing the camera back to Ashley, who scowled at him. He looked at Sam. "I'd like you to leave now."

"Glad to," Sam said, his voice stiff.

As we walked out, a kid tapped me on the shoulder and handed me the memory stick. I stuffed it in my pocket.

CHAPTER 18

ASHLEY

I jumped into the front seat and Bryce didn't argue. His
cheeks were as red as a hot pepper when he slipped in beside Dylan,
pulled his knees up, and hid his face. Dylan turned on his hat light
and patted Bryce on the head, but it didn't help.

I was bummed that we couldn't go into the vug. The way the guy
pumped it up made me feel like we'd almost be going back in time.
Plus, I'd read some stuff on the Internet about gold's history—how
the capitol dome in Denver is made of real gold, and how many
people died trying to strike it rich.

Sam looked in the rearview mirror. "There wasn't a sign, was
there?"

Bryce shook his head vigorously.

"Don't worry about that guy. He's just wrapped a little too tight."

"We didn't even get to see the vug," I said, then wished I hadn't because Bryce looked even more miserable.

As we drove away, I saw the shop owner waving and yelling, but Sam sped off.

Back at the cabin Sam lit the grill. Dylan found the pinball machine and dragged a chair up to it, where he stood trying to make it work. There was no tearing him away from it until dinner was ready.

We didn't make a sound while we ate, except for Dylan, who clicked his hat light on and off and whined about going back to the "Ping-Pong machine." The burgers tasted great, and Sam waited until after I had eaten mine to tell us they were buffalo meat.

"Mmm, buffalo," Dylan said, picking up his burger and bouncing it across his plate like it was running in a field. A few pieces fell on his plate, and he giggled. "He pooped."

That even made Bryce smile.

Sam asked Bryce to help wash the dishes. It would be my turn the next day, so I went downstairs to the computer. Then I remembered I couldn't send Mom the pictures, so I e-mailed her about what had happened. I also told her I hoped her book was going well. I almost explained what had happened with Hayley, but I just couldn't.

What must Hayley have thought about me? Had I blown my chance to tell her about God? I really wanted to, not to bang her over the head, but just tell her what a difference God's made in me. But if I'd watch that kind of stuff, had he made a difference?

Normally my brother and I don't snoop on each other. He doesn't read my diary, and I don't listen on the extension when he talks with his friends. But for some reason I checked Bryce's e-mail, and something in the subject line of one message told me I should read it. It said, "Better watch out."

The return address was Darryl Heckler, which I figured was Boo's dad. I had no idea how Boo had gotten Bryce's address, but the message sent a chill down my back.

Hey, Timberhead—

I meant what I said today. We'll be waiting for you Monday, if not sooner.

You know who

I thought about deleting it. Bryce didn't need to see this, but it might come in handy if Boo ever denied he'd threatened him.

CHAPTER 19

BRYCE

I didn't feel like helping with the dishes, but at least it took my mind off what had happened. Sam washed and I dried.

After Dylan and Ashley were gone, Sam folded his arms, leaned against the sink, and said in his deep voice, "Can I tell you something about people? Most of the time they're in their own little world, me included. If something goes wrong, they'll take it out on somebody, and today that was you. You didn't mean to do anything wrong. I know you've got a good heart."

"He didn't have to treat us that way."

"No, and it was all I could do to keep from telling him what I thought." Sam took the towel from my hand and folded it. "Something's going on at school, isn't it?"

"Why?"

"Your mom said she could tell. Wanted me to find out what it was."

"Nothing I can't handle," I said.

"Well, if you need help, let me know." He went back to washing and told me I was done.

I started downstairs, then turned back. "Sam, I've wanted to ask you this for a long time."

"Go ahead," he said, his hands still in dishwater.

"Why haven't you become a . . . I mean, what keeps you from . . . ?"

"Doing the God thing?"

"Yeah, I mean, you're better than most Christians I know, the way you treat people. And you don't curse—at least in front of Ashley and me. . . ."

"How do you know I'm not a Christian?"

"Mom said you weren't interested."

Sam turned and smiled. His mustache got lost in the wrinkles in his face, and his eyes sparkled. "One of these days we'll have to have a long talk about that. For now, you should know I respect you three and your decision to follow God."

"But what about you?"

He pursed his lips. "Let's just say God and I haven't gotten along too well for a while."

"You mean 'cause your wife and daughter died?"

"That's part of it."

He looked like he had just been hit by an ocean wave, so I decided to drop it. Ever since Ashley and I had become Christians we'd been praying for Sam and Leigh. It seemed like God was doing something in their lives, working somehow, but now wasn't the right time to talk to Sam about it.

Before I headed down the stairs I said, "Thanks."

"For what?"

"For not treating me like a little kid."

"You're welcome."

CHAPTER 20

ASHLEY

While Sam went for a walk with Dylan, Bryce and I tried to find a movie on the satellite. I found a good one about a girl whose horse gets hurt and she has to help it get better so it can race again. Bryce wanted to watch a cheesy show about a bunch of kids who are hired by a spy agency. There were lots of dark outfits and teens climbing things, being sarcastic, and pulling stuff out of their noses. We fought for a few minutes. Then I stormed upstairs to the smaller TV.

The light faded over the mountains, and there was an orange glow shining through the front window. The valley looked like some golden painting you see in museums. Somehow that view made me want to talk to Mom and get the whole Hayley thing out in the open, but I turned on the TV instead.

I clicked around until I found the horse movie. I was at the predictable part where the vet shakes his head and says it's no use and that they'd need to put the horse down when the phone rang. With one eye on the TV I backed to the phone. "Hello?"

Just someone breathing. I heard a car passing in the background. "Mom?" I said.

Silence. Then a click—not the phone hanging up but another sound. A click. I had heard that before. Where?

"Who is this?" I said.

Now I was afraid. I looked out the window for Sam, but he wasn't there. I wished I could send some piercing sound through the phone. "Is that you, Boo? How'd you get our number?"

The line went dead. I put the phone down and slowly walked to the couch. I was standing, staring out the window, when Bryce came to the top of the stairs.

"Who was that?"

I flicked off the TV. "Bryce, I'm scared. They didn't say anything. There was just a clicking sound."

"Maybe it was a wrong number."

"No, they just listened to me. I think it might have been Boo."

"Why?"

I told him about the e-mail and a sick look came over him, like a black cloud rolling over the Front Range.

"Don't tell Sam," Bryce said. "And if it rings again, let me get it."

CHAPTER 21

BRYCE

The TV show had almost made me forget about Boo, but Ashley's telling me about his e-mail brought him back. I could see myself in a body cast, drinking buffalo burgers through a straw, and typing with one toe. The tooth fairy would have to work overtime when Boo got through with me.

"You want to radio Sam and find out where he is?" Ashley said.

"I don't want him to think we're sissies."

Ring.

I jumped two feet off the floor.

Ashley grabbed my arm, trembling. We both looked at the phone, as if that would do any good. The phone didn't have caller ID like the one at home.

It was almost dark. Shadows filled the room, and I turned on a light.

The phone rang again.

"Why don't they leave us alone!" Ashley said.

"Call Sam on the walkie-talkie."

Ashley ran for her jacket. When she pulled out the walkie-talkie, I picked up the phone and pressed the Talk button. "I d-don't care wh-who this is or wh-what you want, b-but you'd b-b-better stop now!"

There was a pause. "Well, if you don't want to talk with me, I'll hang up," my mother said.

"Mom!" I shouted.

Relief came over Ashley's face.

"What's going on up there?" Mom said.

"We just had a prank call."

"Where's Sam?"

After I told her, Ashley took the phone into the other room. She yelped, so I went to see what was wrong. Ashley put a hand over the phone. "Leigh backed The Creep's car into a post and bent his fender."

"She's had her first accident," I said. "How romantic."

Ashley went back to her conversation.

I wished Sam would return, but I didn't want to call him on the walkie-talkie. I don't care how scared you are—there are just some things guys don't do.

Then I had an idea. I pushed the Transmit button. "Sam, it's Bryce. Mom's on the phone if you want to talk to her."

I waited, then heard a click. "Gotcha." Sam sounded out of breath. "We'll be there in a couple minutes. Out."

CHAPTER 22

ASHLEY

Dylan's eyes drooped so I knew he was ready for bed. I carried him upstairs to the loft, put him on the chaise, and covered him up. He started to get up, so I sang his favorite songs—"Twinkle, Twinkle, Little Star," "Hush, Little Baby," and "The Wabash Cannonball," which he calls "the train song."

When I got back downstairs, Sam was making popcorn and Bryce had found some board games. The three of us decided on Sorry. Bryce and I ganged up on Sam, and he made a big deal about being sent back to his circle. As we played and drank sodas, Bryce and I had a burping contest, and Sam gave us points for the loudest and longest. Mom wouldn't have appreciated that as much as we did, and to be honest it was kind of gross, but it felt good to laugh. It was something our real dad would have done with us.

Finally, Sam said he had to go to bed. "But there's one thing I have to say before I go."

"What?" Bryce said.

Sam stood, spread his arms dramatically, then opened his mouth and won the contest. It was the deepest, longest burp in the history of burpdom. It sounded like a minute-long growl of a wounded lion.

Bryce and I looked at each other, dazzled, then laughed till I thought I'd never breathe again.

"No fair!" I said. "You were holding that all this time!"

At the top of the stairs, Sam turned. Bryce and I held up two signs that said 10 and he smiled. "Get some sleep. I have some fun stuff planned for tomorrow."

CHAPTER 23

BRYCE

My sides still hurt from laughing when Ashley and I went downstairs to watch more TV before going to bed. We found a classic movie channel showing *The African Queen*. Our real dad had shown it to us when we were little, and it brought back memories of snuggling with him and closing our eyes when Humphrey Bogart came out of the water with leeches all over his body.

"Remember watching this with Dad?" Ashley said.

I nodded. "I feel kind of bad for having such a good time with Sam. It's almost like we're betraying Dad."

"I was thinking the same thing." Ashley sat up and looked out the window. The room was dark, and the television reflected in the window.

"What is it?"

"Someone's out there," she whispered.

"You're trying to scare me—"

"No, seriously. I thought I saw somebody."

I turned the TV off. The lower floor was only slightly underground, so we could easily see outside. Sam had left the outside light on, and it was snowing softly. A couple of inches had fallen already. The light shone a few feet from the house, but the rest was pitch-black.

"If somebody's out there," I said, "they could go right over the side of the cliff."

"There!" Ashley pointed out the side window. "See that orange glow?"

I couldn't see anything.

"Now I know what I heard on the phone!" she said. "Remember I said I heard a clicking sound during the phone call?"

"Yeah?"

"It was a cigarette lighter. You know, the big metal kind Uncle Terry used?"

Uncle Terry had lived back in Indiana and was a chain smoker. He had died the year before we moved to Colorado. Every time we visited, we had to sit outside so we could breathe. He was a wonderful uncle, always inviting us to the farm to pick pumpkins or corn or whatever was in season, but hugging him was like embracing an ashtray. I remembered his big cigarette lighter with a dragon on the front of it. The smell of it fascinated me. He said it was butane, whatever that is.

I saw a glow near some trees at the side of the house. It grew orange, then died, then grew orange again.

Whoever was out there was smoking, and whoever it was had his eyes on us.

CHAPTER 24

Gavin Winkler peered inside the cabin. He had watched the twins play their games and laugh with their father. He tried to remember doing the same thing with his dad when he was a kid, but he couldn't come up with a single memory. His father had gone to prison when Gavin was 10, and they hadn't seen each other since. The scene inside the cabin turned his stomach.

He wished they'd get to bed. He had work to do. Get in, get that camera and its memory stick, and get out.

Gavin took another puff of his cigarette as the kids moved to the basement. When the TV flicked on, Gavin cursed. He was tempted to go in while they were downstairs, but he couldn't be sure the father would be asleep yet. He'd found a security system on the cabin and easily disarmed it. He'd be in and out in a couple of minutes.

If they would just get out of the way.

CHAPTER 25

ASHLEY

Bryce and I raced upstairs and woke Sam, trying not to disturb Dylan.

Sam bolted out of bed in his pajamas and rushed downstairs. I was going to show him where I thought the prowler was, but he immediately threw his coat on, slipped on his shoes, grabbed a flashlight, and headed outside.

"What if he gets jumped?" Bryce said.

I peeked out the window. Sam traipsed through the brush and trees, where we had seen the glowing cigarette, his flashlight casting a wide beam. I held my breath.

He stopped and bent over, then continued around the house. Bryce and I followed him from window to window. Bryce grabbed the phone, obviously ready to dial 911. I wondered if they even had that service out here in the woods and how long it would take the police to come.

When Sam made it all the way around the house, he sprinted down the long driveway. All we could see was the flashlight beam bouncing off trees and rocks and snow.

Bryce gave me a look. "You think he saw something?"

I shrugged, but I knew one thing: we were alone. Whoever was out there could have been hoping that Sam would go outside.

"Is the downstairs door locked?" Bryce said.

"You were the last one in—"

"No way, you were!"

We argued, then crept downstairs. As we passed the spooky picture of the woman dressed in red, it took all the nerve I had to check the lock. Then we rushed back upstairs, and I tripped over something and banged my knee. The pinball machine went wild, beeping and buzzing and lighting the darkness.

Something banged above us. Bryce helped me up.

"Sam?" I yelled.

"It's me," he called. "Everything's okay."

He dusted the snow from his pants and kicked off his shoes. "You two playing pinball while I was gone?" He smiled.

I held my knee. "Why did you run down the driveway?"

"Thought I heard a car, but I couldn't find any tracks." Sam showed us a cigarette butt. "But I did find this at the side of the house near a window. Still fresh."

CHAPTER 26

BRYCE

The cigarette proved we were right. Ashley and I knew someone had been watching the cabin. But why?

Sam carried Dylan to Ashley's room, the one with the bunk beds,
while Ashley and I turned on every light in the house. The three of
us slept in the bunk room, while Sam slept just outside on the couch
he pulled near the door. I had a hard time getting to sleep, listening to
the wind whistle through the trees. Twice I thought I saw something
outside our window and Sam came in. It was just snow.

The next morning a good 8 to 10 inches of new snow lay on the
ground. Any footprints or tire tracks had been covered.

Sam called the sheriff, but someone put him on hold. Finally, a deputy took the information.

After a few minutes, Sam hung up, and I could tell he was ticked. "They said they wouldn't be able to get to it today," he said. "Something's going on over there."

Dylan came out of the bedroom carrying his blanket, rubbing his eyes, and yawning. "How did I get down here?"

Dylan could sleep through anything. Mom said Ashley and I had been the same way when we were his age, but I couldn't believe it.

"They don't have time for a prowler?" Ashley said. "Whoever it was could have . . ." She glanced at Dylan and stopped.

"What's a prowler?" he said.

Sam poured a cup of coffee and started the stove. "Okay, it's time for fun. We have fresh snow out there, and we're taking advantage of it. There's a great slope at a resort not far from here. We'll rent some skis or snowboards for you two, and we'll use the tubes."

Dylan's face lit up. "Can I go?" He was used to being left behind.

Sam flashed a smile and nodded.

CHAPTER 27

ASHLEY

I don't like lots of greasy food, but the bacon and sausage Sam made that morning went so well with the eggs and pancakes that I had to stop myself before I got sick. Bryce pushed his plate back too, his mouth full of pancakes and syrup. Sam found plastic bags, and we saved the rest for the next morning.

Bryce and I helped Dylan get dressed in several layers of clothes. Just when we got his boots and gloves on he said he had to go to the bathroom. Sometimes life's like that.

Sam handed us our walkie-talkies, but after the night before, I didn't want to go off on our own. I wanted to stay near Sam.

He wanted to hear the news, so he found a crackly radio station playing country music. Bryce gave me a look like he was going to die. We both hated country music back in Illinois, but I had to admit that some of the singers were starting to grow on me now.

The music ended and a man with a voice like a frog told the song titles. He identified himself as Tiny Woods and said he'd be on the air until noon. "And if you haven't heard, the big news this morning is the robbery last night at Gold Town. We have the sheriff on the line now."

I glanced at Sam with my mouth open.

He just shook his head.

"What do you think they took?" Bryce said from the backseat.

The radio squealed until Tiny flipped a switch. "Sounds like somebody struck it rich last night, Sheriff."

"That's right, Tiny," the sheriff said in a cooing voice that let us know he knew the man well. "At about six o'clock last night, as they were shutting down for the evening, the owner of the gold nugget noticed something strange. It was a lot lighter than the original."

Sam pulled to the side of the road and turned up the radio.

"Bathroom," Dylan said.

Sam put up a hand. "In a minute. I want to hear this."

"So someone replaced the real one with a fake?" Tiny said.

"It appears so, Tiny."

"I imagine you're pretty busy with this," Tiny said.

"We have all our people on it, and we're going to catch the person who's responsible."

"Any leads?"

"No. We don't even know when the switch took place. But there's a reward for anyone with information that leads to an arrest."

"You mean we were looking at fake gold?" Bryce said.

Sam stroked his chin. "Let's head over to Gold Town. Dylan can use the restroom, and we'll tell them we were there."

CHAPTER 28

BRYCE

I was glad to see police cars when we pulled into Gold Town. I took Dylan to the outside toilet near the building while Ashley went with Sam to the front.

Through a vent in the back, I glimpsed someone walking through the brush behind the bathroom. I wondered if it might be an officer hunting for clues.

When Dylan said, "Done!" I helped him wash his hands, and we walked outside. Behind the bathroom I saw the kid who had handed me the camera's memory stick the day before. I guessed he was the shop owner's son. They looked a little alike. I was wearing the same pants as the day before, so I patted my pocket and felt the memory stick.

I was about to say something to him when I noticed Ashley and Sam heading toward the SUV. I could tell by the way Sam walked that he was mad.

"What happened?" I said as I snapped the belt around Dylan's car seat.

"They wouldn't even talk to us," Ashley said. "Sam said we were here yesterday, but the deputy just took our number and told us to go."

"You'd think they'd want all the info they could get," I said.

"Guess it doesn't work that way out here," Sam said.

When we arrived at the ski resort, Ashley said she wanted to go tubing with Sam and Dylan, which made me think she was still scared. I have to admit that I was too, so I decided to join them. I didn't want the memory stick to get smashed while I was tubing, so I pulled it out of my pocket and stuck it in the slot behind Ashley's seat.

Dylan was allowed up the hill only with Sam. Sam held him tightly on his lap, and when they took off Dylan squealed. I had never heard such a shrill sound.

Ashley and I followed in a tube train, with me holding her feet. It's weird for it to be sunny and dry one day and snowing the next, but that's how it is in Colorado. The snow swished into my face, and I had to close my eyes. By the time I made it to the bottom, I was covered and loving every minute.

"Again!" Dylan screamed. "Again!"

The next time I went by myself and was surprised at how fast the tube went. Ashley and I had a contest to see how far we could slide. The run ended in a steep snowbank, but if you veered left you could go all the way to the tree line.

The third time down I made it past the snowbank and kept going until I stopped near the winding road. I stood and waved at Ashley so she could see how far I'd gone.

A green car slowed to my left. The driver looked straight at me. Something about the man made my skin crawl. I was sure I'd seen him before. But where?

I hurried back up the hill, searching for Sam and Ashley. When I glanced over my shoulder, the car was speeding away from the resort.

CHAPTER 29

ASHLEY

Bryce's story about the driver of the green car made me nervous again. I kept looking for people behind trees, waiting to jump out at me. The only thing that kept me from running back to our Land Cruiser was Dylan's squeals of delight. Sam let me have a turn with Dylan, and as we raced down the mountain, he stuck out his arms as if he were flying. It almost felt like we were.

I was relieved when Sam suggested we get something to eat. We found a restaurant at the resort, and I ordered the buffet. Though Mom can't stand salad bars, I love them. I like the dressing, croutons, cheese, sunflower seeds, and veggies. Here, you could get any kind of meat you wanted, from fried chicken to buffalo, and any kind of potato, fish, and lots of steamed vegetables.

Dylan stared at my plate when I got back to the table, and his eyes grew wide. He has a way of wanting whatever is not on his plate. No matter how much food he already has, if he sees cottage cheese, even on TV, he wants it.

"I want cartoons," he said.

Sam grinned. "You want what?"

"Cartoons."

"Croutons," Bryce said.

Sam chuckled. "Leigh used to call them wood chips."

"Cartoons!" Dylan chortled.

Sam faced him. "When you finish what you have, I'll get you some, okay?"

I could tell it wasn't okay with Dylan, but it got his eyes back onto his plate. Then he wanted a red drink instead of a yellow one, and I told Sam I would get it.

I felt sorry for Sam. He had taken us as his children, but I knew he missed his own wife and daughter. I had seen their pictures in Leigh's room. The little girl looked sweet in the heart-shaped frame Mom had given Leigh.

Dylan was a lot of work, even for Mom, and though Sam had seemed to win him over with the Chunky Monkey and the trip to the cabin, I was surprised Dylan hadn't cried for Mom during the night. He usually clung to her.

When Dylan wailed over a piece of celery, Sam took a deep breath. "You two ready?"

Bryce's plate wasn't even half empty, but we looked at each other and said, "Okay" at the same time.

We weren't in the SUV three minutes before Dylan fell asleep. "Nap management," my mom calls it.

Early in the afternoon we got back to the cabin, and I was ready for a nap myself.

The chain was down on the driveway and Sam stopped. "Thought I put that back before we left."

"Maybe it fell," Bryce said.

Sam handed the keys to Bryce, who went to unlock the cabin. Getting Dylan from the Land Cruiser to his bed without waking him is tricky and almost never works unless it's a straight shot from the SUV to the sheets.

"Sam!" Bryce yelled from the front door. "You'd better come see this!"

Dylan woke up and Sam stared at Bryce.

"Sorry, but somebody broke in."

CHAPTER 30

BRYCE

It looked like a tornado had hit the cabin. The kitchen table was on its side, food all over the floor. Cushions had been taken from the chairs and the large couch near the fireplace.

"Don't touch anything," Sam said as he carried Dylan inside.

I stepped over the debris, went to Ashley's bedroom, and found the mattresses off the bunk beds. It was the same in my room and upstairs. Downstairs, things were even worse. The computer cabinet lay on the floor, the computer gone.

Ashley took Dylan upstairs to keep him away from the broken glass.

Sam pulled out his cell phone and dialed the local police. I could tell by the way he spoke that he wasn't happy with the people on the other end.

He hung up and dialed another number. "Jack, it's Sam . . . yeah, we made it fine, but we just got back from a little adventure and the place has been ransacked. More mess than real damage, though there's a window downstairs that'll need some work. The computer is gone. . . . No, we had it locked."

Sam paused and frowned. He told the owner of the cabin that he had contacted the police.

"Is the guy mad at us?" I said after he hung up.

"I don't think so. Upset, I guess. I would be too. He may know someone over at the police station who can come out and take a look."

"Who would do this?" I said.

Sam pursed his lips. "If it was a thief, he would have taken more than just the computer. Everything else is still here. Whoever it was was searching for something in particular."

By the time the police got to the cabin a couple of hours later, I was going crazy trying to keep Dylan from going outside and messing up the footprints, but we also didn't want him to get hurt inside. The pinball machine kept him busy. I was glad the robber hadn't trashed it.

Ashley came downstairs to watch Dylan when the deputy arrived. He was skinny and sort of young, with a patchy mustache. Ashley said it was the same deputy they saw at Gold Town. He took notes but didn't seem to want to be here, like he was playing in a minor-league baseball game when he could have been in the majors.

"Any news on the gold?" I said.

The deputy glanced at me, then went on writing.

Sam raised an eyebrow and frowned. He seemed to be saying, "This guy isn't as interested in our problem as we'd like him to be, but it's not your fault."

The deputy finally looked up. "Anything to add, Sport?"

There may be some 13-year-olds who like to be called Sport, but I'm not one of them. People use nicknames with kids because they can't remember their names or don't care to know them. Plus, we used to have a neighbor whose dog was named Sport.

I told the deputy about Boo Heckler, what he had said about our ATVs, and about the e-mail.

Sam looked troubled so I gave him a smirk that I hoped he would read as, "I'm sorry I didn't tell you—I wanted to handle it myself, but now it's just too big."

"Think he could have followed you up here?" the deputy said.

"Somebody would have had to drive him. The guy we saw out the window last night was smoking, and I know Boo smokes."

"You sure it was a man?" the deputy said.

I shrugged. "Could have been a man or a woman, I guess."

"Okay." The deputy slapped his notepad shut. "Call us if you need us."

"What are we supposed to do?" Sam said.

"I'd patch the window and clean up this place."

"No fingerprints?"

The deputy sighed. "Sorry."

CHAPTER 31

ASHLEY

Bryce and I helped Sam clean up. He swept the glass into a
trash can and put it outside on the patio. Dylan just played pinball.
As long as we heard the ding-ding of the machine, we knew he was
okay.

As I worked, I thought about Mom. I kicked myself for not telling
her the truth about what had happened at Hayley's. Inside my head
was just like this cabin—all messed up. I had a feeling that no matter
how much I tried to clean myself up, there was no way I could
without talking to Mom.

I got out my journal, and for the first time in a long time, I had no candle to burn while I wrote. But sometimes you have to just go ahead and write.

> Dear God,
>
> I'm really sorry about what happened at Hayley's house. I feel so bad that I didn't say something and stop the movie or at least walk out. Please forgive me and help me talk to Mom about it. And please help me talk to Hayley too. I want her to become a believer in you.
> Please help me find some way to talk to her. And thank you for forgiving me.

I signed the entry with an *A*. I never end my journals to God with *amen*, because it would make things seem too official. When I journal to God, it's just me and him.

I flipped to the beginning of the notebook and found another entry. The words made tears come to my eyes. It's funny how a journal can change in only a few pages. The first entry described a day Dad had spent with us.

He had taken us to his office in downtown Chicago, then to Lake Michigan. Mom, who was feeling sick, had stayed behind. With the wind in our faces we walked along the lakeshore, looking at the tall buildings across Lake Shore Drive and out at the lake on the other side. The water didn't seem to end, just like the ocean. Gulls danced on the sand, picking at trash. Cars sped along Lake Shore Drive, but when you looked at the water it didn't feel like you were near a huge city.

"Why do you have to go away, Dad?" Bryce had said without a hint of a stutter. "Can't you stay?"

"It won't be a very long trip," Dad said.

"It's halfway on the other side of the world," I said.

He sat us on the sand and hugged us tight. "I brought you here to-day because I wanted to tell you something very important, and I want you to always remember where you found out."

"Found out what?" Bryce said.

He pulled out a video camera and turned it on, pointing it at our faces. "You two are about to go through one of the biggest changes in your entire lives."

"This isn't the big-boy talk, is it?" Bryce said.

"What big-boy talk?" Dad said.

"You know, the one about your body changing and that 'poogerty' stuff?"

"Puberty," I said.

Dad stifled a laugh and hugged us again. "No, this is a different kind of change."

A few months earlier Dad had become a Christian and started going to Bible studies and church. Mom wasn't interested, but we could all see a change in him. It wasn't like he stopped getting drunk or robbing banks, because he had never done that. The best way to explain it is that he seemed to open a door to a room he didn't know existed, and it changed everything. I could see it in his eyes. When he looked at you, he didn't look past you to the next thing. He really looked.

He pointed toward the lake. "See the horizon, where the water meets the sky? I want you to be looking right there when I tell you this. Are you looking?"

"Yeah," we said, both of us eager to hear what he was going to say.

"Bryce, you're going to be a big brother. Ashley, you're going to be a big sister."

Bryce leaned forward and stared at me, his mouth open. I couldn't hide my excitement either. We had asked Mom and Dad for a little brother or sister—me for a girl, Bryce for a boy.

Dad took the video back home and showed it to Mom. Big tears streamed down her cheeks as she watched.

Every time I look at water now, I think of Dad and that day. What he didn't tell us, and what he didn't know, was that he wouldn't be around to help us become a good big brother or sister.

I flipped to June 23.

> We just heard on the news that a plane going to Europe went down in the ocean. They think it's Dad's plane and that it might have been a terrorist attack.

The next few entries talked about the funeral and the days after.

> It rained at the funeral today. It was weird not actually seeing Dad's body. We all sat in front of an empty coffin with his picture on top. I don't remember much about what the pastor said or what verses he used. I just remember trying not to cry and being a miserable failure.
>
> They had a memorial service at Dad's church, and people got up and talked about him. They all looked at us, cried, and told us what a good man our dad had been. Something about it made me angry. I don't need these people to tell me what my dad was like. I knew him. He was the one who read to me, tucked me in at night, and took us to movies. I didn't even want to be there, but Mom said it was important for "closure"—whatever that means. Wasn't it enough "closure" that they closed the lid and buried the coffin?

Then came the entries about the first pictures on TV of the plane wreckage floating on the waves. Mom had kept us from watching the video at first. Then she let us. Some families actually got in boats and went out to sea to toss wreaths. I asked her why we couldn't do that, but she didn't answer. Instead, she took some dirt from Dad's grave, used it to plant flowers, and gave the pots to friends. She also put some throughout the house. A few days later all the flowers had died.

A month later some news crews came to interview Mom. We listened from upstairs as she tried to describe her feelings and tell what it was like to move on with life. That's the weird thing. At first it feels like everybody in the world cares about you, and then they all just go back about their business like nothing's happened.

I closed the journal and thought of watching Dad shave right before his last trip. I wish we would have gone to the airport that day and said good-bye. We all thought he was coming home. Nobody on that plane came home.

Now I think of Dad in heaven, watching us. I don't know if that's how it works, if he can actually see us. Somewhere in the New Testament—I think it's Hebrews—it says that we are surrounded by a huge crowd of witnesses. I like to think of my dad in that crowd, cheering us on. I don't know if he's there or if he's off building something or maybe worshiping God.

Part of me thinks he's just standing by Jesus. Another part of me thinks he's standing at the horizon, where the water meets the sky, waiting for us.

CHAPTER 32

BRYCE

"Do you hear that?" Sam said.

Ashley was off by herself, and I was helping Sam clean up the living room and kitchen.

"I don't hear anything," I said.

"Exactly," Sam said. "What do you think Dylan's up to?"

"Dylan!" I whispered.

We bolted downstairs. Sam had duct taped a piece of cardboard over the broken window, but still it was about 10 degrees colder down there than upstairs.

I was about to yell for Dylan when Sam put a hand on my shoulder and pointed toward the pinball machine. Dylan had both hands atop it, his head (which is about two times too big for his body) resting against one flipper button. As he breathed, the flippers clicked, but there was no ball to hit. His little eyelids were shut, but his mouth was open just enough for his tongue to stick through. His shirtsleeve had a drool stain the size of a quarter.

How he stood there without his knees giving way, I'll never know.

Sam ran for his cell phone and snapped a picture. This was a sure winner for one of those funny kid contests. I went upstairs to get Ashley, but she was on a bed with an arm over her face. Her journal was nearby, so I left her alone and crept back downstairs.

"What should we do with him?" Sam said. I could tell he wasn't just saying it. He really wanted my opinion.

"I don't think he's ever gone to sleep standing up before," I said. "Mom always says we should leave him wherever he rolls to a stop."

Sam smiled and grabbed a pillow from the couch. "In case he slides down, this'll break his fall."

CHAPTER 33

ASHLEY

I wiped my eyes so Bryce and Sam wouldn't notice I had been crying. They were at the kitchen table, a yellow legal pad in front of Bryce.

Sam said they were trying to figure things out. "I wonder if we should head back home."

I agreed with him, but I didn't want to be a chicken.

"Here's what we have so far," Bryce said, sliding the pad over to me.

I read the list silently.

1. Prowler seen last night outside the house.

2. Suspicious car at the ski resort. Could be watching us.
3. Cabin ransacked while we were gone—what are they looking for?
4. Boo Heckler made threats.

Sam plugged his laptop into the high-speed modem. The robbers had missed it in his suitcase. "Do you know Boo's father's name?"

Bryce shook his head. "Why?"

"I want to see if he's at home."

"I think it's Darryl," I said, remembering the e-mail message. I looked at Bryce. "I don't know if calling him is a good idea."

"The cabin's phone doesn't come up on caller ID," Sam said.

He pulled up all the Hecklers in Red Rock. "It'd probably be better if one of you asked for him. If I call and ask if he's home, they'll probably ask who it is."

"I'll do it," I said.

"No, let me," Bryce said.

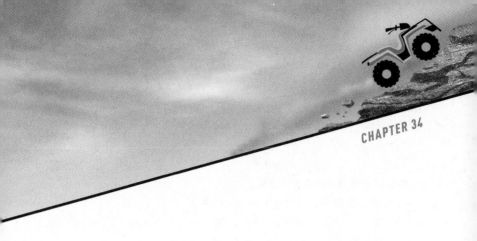

CHAPTER 34

BRYCE

I dialed the number slowly, then hit the End button. "What if Boo answers?"

"Say you got a wrong number," Ashley said.

"Just hand it to me," Sam said.

I thought Boo should have some kind of special toll-free number like 1-800-SCARY. My hands started sweating, and I worried about stuttering. My family thinks my stuttering doesn't bother me, but it does. A lot.

The line was busy. I wiped my hands on my pants.

"Should we put the stolen gold on the clue list?" Ashley said.

Sam nodded. "It's a long shot, but it could be related."

I added it and wrote that the person outside the house was a smoker. We also wrote down the description of the car I saw at the ski resort.

"Try it again," Ashley said.

This time it rang. Before I could hang up, a girl answered, probably one of Boo's sisters.

"Uh . . . yeah . . . is A-a-aron there?"

"Hang on." She screamed his name without covering the phone, and I handed it to Sam.

"Hello, Aaron," he said in his deep voice. "How are you?" Sam grinned at me. "Well, I'm part of a group of concerned parents at the school."

Sam paused and held the phone away from his ear. Because the handset was turned up, Ashley and I both heard Boo.

"I didn't do anything," Boo said. "Who are you, anyway?"

"As I said, just a concerned parent. And I'm calling for a very important reason."

"What's that?"

I held a hand over my mouth. Ashley turned red.

"Have you been home all weekend?"

"Yeah, why?"

"Well," Sam said, trying to hold his own laughter, "we're making sure all of our top students are getting enough rest this weekend so they'll be ready for the CATs on Monday. Are you planning any trips or sleepovers?"

"Not that I know of," Boo said, his voice a little calmer. "I'm on the list of top students?"

As far as I knew, Boo had never made the honor roll.

"Well, actually, any person who doesn't take the test gets a zero, so we really need everyone there," Sam said, then put his hand over the mouthpiece so Boo wouldn't hear his chuckles.

"Tell whoever wants to know that I'll be there," Boo said. "I have to be there anyway."

"Oh?" Sam said.

"Yeah, got a score to settle."

A shiver ran down my spine. This wasn't funny anymore.

"You know, Aaron, I've heard you've made it a little difficult on a couple of students at school. If I were you, I'd concentrate on my studies and cut out the extracurricular activities. You get my drift?"

Boo paused. "Extra what?"

"The fighting and bullying."

"Hey, who is this?"

"Just a friendly reminder," Sam said. "Good luck on the CATs Monday."

CHAPTER 35

ASHLEY

I burst out laughing, but I could tell Bryce was upset.

"If Boo is telling the truth about being home, he wasn't the one outside," Bryce said.

Sam paced. "What happened back in Gold Town? Did you two buy anything or pick up anything?"

"You mean like a souvenir?" I said.

"Anything."

"The only thing we came out of there with that we didn't walk in with was the miner's hat you bought Dylan," Bryce said. "Unless you bought something, Ash."

I closed my eyes and tried to remember. "We walked in, got in line—Dylan put on the hat, you took the picture, the guy erased the photos, and then they asked us to leave."

"Wait," Bryce said. He put a hand in his pocket. "When I dropped the camera, the memory stick flew out. A kid handed it to me." He frowned, then snapped his fingers. "I know where it is. I'll be right back."

"Where are you going?" Sam said.

"The stick is in the back of the SUV—"

"But what good will that do?" I said.

"Pictures. Maybe this has something to do with the pictures. The guy at Gold Town erased the camera but not the stick."

CHAPTER 36

BRYCE

The Land Cruiser was locked. The sun was still high, but the pine trees cast long shadows. I ran back inside, and as soon as I opened the door, Sam tossed me his keys before I could even ask for them. They say great minds think alike.

Once in the SUV I crawled over the front seat, opened the flap behind it, and found the memory stick. When I locked the door and closed it, I heard something behind me. A car? Someone in the woods?

"H-hello?" I called.

Something fluttered overhead, and my heart jumped into my

throat. I had the same feeling the summer before on a 3-2 count with the bases loaded in the bottom of the seventh. And the time Ashley and I set up the bike jump in our front yard in Illinois—I had the same feeling just as I was about to go airborne.

I dashed to the house and didn't turn around until I was inside.

CHAPTER 37

ASHLEY

Bryce was out of breath and looked like he had seen a herd of ghosts. He hurried over with the memory stick and put it on the table. "I heard someone out there," he said.

Sam peered outside. "A car?"

Bryce shook his head. "I don't know."

Sam opened the door. "Hey!" His voice echoed off the hillside. Snow fell from a pine tree nearby and whooshed as it slapped branches on the way down. Sam stood watching and finally closed the door. "Go get your camera, Ashley."

I looked all over the cabin. When I told Sam I couldn't find it any-where, he gritted his teeth. "Must've been what they were after."

He plugged the memory stick into his computer and brought up the shots on the screen. The first showed Bryce mugging, as usual, tugging his ears and sticking out his tongue. The second was me pulling my hair out to both sides, doing the helicopter. I thought we should go to the thumbnails so we could see all of them, but Sam said he wanted to see them in order.

When he reached the last picture, we hovered over the computer, studying the shot. The gold nugget was out of focus at the front.

"Looks like the real thing to me," Bryce said.

Sam went back to a shot I had taken outside the trailer before we went inside. "What's this?" He enlarged it, and I noticed two men at the right of the picture. One had his back turned to the camera. He was talking with another man wearing a hat.

"Is there a way to zoom in on that guy's face?" Bryce said.

Sam clicked the mouse and moved the cursor around. I didn't know being a pilot made you good at computers, but he really had skill.

The man's face filled the screen. Blondish red hair stuck out of a red hat with a *C* on it.

"Cincinnati," Bryce said.

"How do you know?" I said. "Could be Chicago or Cleveland, couldn't it?"

He shook his head. "Wrong color. Wrong shape *C*. It's Cincinnati all right."

"Could they have been looking for this picture?" I said.

"How would they even know it existed?" Sam said. "Seems strange, unless . . ."

"Unless what?" Bryce said.

Something banged downstairs.

CHAPTER 38

BRYCE

My heart raced as I followed Sam downstairs, Ashley right
behind me. The pinball machine was going wild. Dylan was flipping
flippers and smiling from ear to ear. I was sure relieved. We watched
him awhile, then left him to have his fun.

Back upstairs Sam studied the picture again. "We'd better take
this to the police."

"They're probably too busy," Ashley said.

I felt really important. To think that we might help solve a gold
heist with a picture . . .

"Know how to copy the pictures to my computer?" Sam said.

"No problem," I said.

Sam went downstairs to pry Dylan from the pinball machine, and Ashley went to her room. I copied the pictures, then logged on to our family Web site. I typed in Mom's e-mail address and attached the pictures so she could see the cabin.

Ashley came back just as the power went out and the house went dark. The only thing that gave any light was Sam's laptop computer, which was running on the battery.

Dylan cried out, but I couldn't tell if he was scared or just mad that the pinball machine didn't work anymore. I heard Sam shush him. "I'm here, big guy," he said.

The front door flew open, and a thin man hurried in. From the light outside I could see that he wore camouflage pants and a tan jacket. He had a *C* on his hat. Ashley screamed, and the man cursed at her.

Before I could do anything, he rushed me and I slid off the chair without thinking. Ashley ran to the stairs, calling for Sam. But the man wasn't after us. He seized the computer and made for the door.

I scrambled to my feet. From the top of the stairs something shot like a cannon and hit the man, sending him sprawling. He dropped the computer.

Sam had sprung through the air like a cat and overpowered the man. He scooped up the computer and memory stick, grabbed Ashley who was holding Dylan, and shouted, "Get to the SUV, quick!"

We raced outside, expecting the man to come flying out any second.

"Give me the keys!" Sam said, gripping a door handle.

I patted my pockets. "I don't have them!"

"You brought them out to get the memory stick!"

I looked inside the Land Cruiser and my stomach fell. There were the keys, on the backseat.

CHAPTER 39

ASHLEY

Dylan was pale and shaking in my arms as he buried his head in my neck. I held him tight, keeping an eye on the cabin, ready to run into the woods if the intruder came out.

"Got to break the window," Sam said.

"Call the police!" Bryce said.

Sam looked at the cabin. "My cell phone's inside."

"You can't go back in," I said.

Sam put the computer on the hood of the Land Cruiser and jammed the memory stick in his pocket. "Listen, if that guy gets past me, let him have the computer. Run that way. Promise?"

"Promise," Bryce said. "Hurry!"

I wanted to go with him, to tell him to be careful, to tell him I loved him. But he was through the door and gone. I held Dylan tighter, closed my eyes, and prayed.

CHAPTER 40

BRYCE

I wondered if we were losing our second dad. I couldn't believe I'd left the keys in the SUV.

Ashley said, "We're going to be okay."

"That guy could kill him."

Seconds ticked by. Something moved to the right of the cabin.

Ashley whispered, "Look at that!"

A deer walked slowly at the edge of the trees. It glanced at us, dipped its head, picked at something on the ground, and kept moving. Suddenly, it jerked its head and leaped into the woods.

Sam burst through the door, and I was never so glad to see him in my life. I'd never noticed how athletic he was. He moved like the deer, loping over the yard and reaching the driver's-side door. He grabbed a rock and smashed the window.

"What about the guy?" I said.

"Still on the floor." Sam reached through the shattered glass to unlock the SUV.

Dylan squirmed. "Nuh-uh," he said, pointing over my shoulder. "He's right there."

CHAPTER 41

ASHLEY

I whirled to see the thin man stagger through the door, waving the long metal poker from the fireplace. I grabbed the computer, and we all jumped in the Land Cruiser, Dylan and me in the back.

By the time Sam got the key in the ignition, the guy was at the SUV, raising the poker over his head.

I pressed back in the seat, but in the next second I lurched forward as Sam started the engine, slammed the Land Cruiser in reverse, and floored it. The man fell.

Snow and mud flew from the tires as Sam spun backward toward the road, slipping and sliding down the driveway.

"The chain!" I said.

Sam slid to a stop and bolted from the SUV.

The man ran toward us, skidding along the path, still holding the poker.

I closed my eyes, hoping this was all a bad dream, but when I opened them, the guy was still coming.

Sam unlatched the chain and jumped back in the Land Cruiser, spinning around in the road before finally regaining control. "Ashley," he said, "get Dylan in his car seat."

We bounced around so much, it was all I could do to finally get Dylan buckled.

"Look," Bryce said, pointing to a thicket of trees. A green car sat by the road. The man raced toward it. Sam drove fast, but the road was snow covered and slick.

We skidded around a corner. I could see jagged rocks below us. There was nothing between us and the cliff but trees that hugged the edge of the road.

"Why do they want that picture so much?" I said.

"Must have something to do with the gold," Bryce said. "Think he'll leave us alone if we give him the memory stick?"

"I'm not giving him anything," Sam said.

Wind blasted through the broken window. I unbuckled and rooted around in the back until I found a blanket to drape over Dylan and me. My teeth were doing a tap dance because none of us had coats on. I found another blanket and tried to plug the open window, but it flew out.

We came to a fork in the road, and Sam turned left onto Gold Camp Road.

"They'll expect us to go toward town where the police station is," Sam said, "but we're going home."

CHAPTER 42

Gavin Winkler drove wildly. No sign of the man and the kids. His head felt light from the conk the man had given him and he tasted blood. The guy knew what he was doing. Former military, Gavin guessed. He clicked on his handheld radio. "They got away. They're heading down the mountain."

"Did they see you?" the other man said angrily.

"Guy came out of nowhere. They could have gone through my wallet if they wanted to."

Winkler came to a fork in the road and slowed.

"Take care of him," the other man said over the radio.

"I don't even know which way they went," Winkler said.

"How about you, Travis? Where are you?"

"Other side of Gold Camp tunnel," Travis said.

"Good. Gavin, stay on the main road. Travis will take Gold Camp. Don't let them get away."

CHAPTER 43

BRYCE

Why did I have to lock the keys in the SUV? I'm always doing stupid things or saying stupid stuff.

"I almost got you killed," I said.

Sam clapped a hand on my knee and seemed to force a smile. "We're going to be okay."

"I think we lost the guy," Ashley said from the backseat.

"Who's that?" Dylan said, pointing to the front.

A pickup truck barreled toward us and swerved into our lane.

Sam grimaced. "Oh no." He jerked the Land Cruiser around the truck, but the driver pulled a U-turn and followed.

If only we hadn't come up here. If only Ashley hadn't taken that picture. If only I hadn't gone to Boo's school. If only Dad hadn't gotten on that plane . . .

But there was nothing I could do to change any of that now. One of these days I would have to quit wishing away the "if only's" and stand up to them.

The pickup following us made Boo's threats seem like nothing. "Let's get these guys, Sam," I said.

CHAPTER 44

ASHLEY

The truck gained on us. I had my arm around Dylan's car seat and hoped he didn't know what was going on. My fingers trembled as I gave him his miner's hat and helped him turn on the light.

I prayed silently. *Please, God, help us get out of this. You know how scared we are.*

Then I prayed God would let the truck run off the road or crash into a tree. Before you decide that's not a very nice thing to pray, you should look in the Psalms where David asks God to break his enemies' teeth and kill them all. The Bible will surprise you.

I missed Mom. She was miles away and didn't even know we were in trouble.

Sam handed me his cell phone and told me to dial 911. I wanted to call Mom, but I punched the three numbers. Nothing happened.

We went into a tunnel and everything went dark. When we came out, we hit a straight stretch and Sam floored it. Still the truck drew closer.

I hit Redial and the phone stayed dead. Finally it rang.

"911, this is McLarty. What is your emergency?"

"A truck's chasing us and we need help! We're on Gold Camp Road—"

"Sorry, ma'am, you're breaking up. What's the nature of your emergency?"

"Gold Camp Road!" I shouted. "We're coming up on a reservoir."

"Sorry, I didn't hear that. What is your location?"

The phone cut out. I dialed again, but Sam said, "We're in a dead spot." I didn't like the sound of that.

Most of the snow had melted from the road so we went faster. The truck was about a football field behind us. A sign showed a curve ahead with a suggested speed of 20 miles an hour. Sam yelled for us to hang on. We raced around the curve doing at least 60, and I thought the Land Cruiser was going to fly off the road. I prayed the truck would.

My mouth was dry as cotton. A funny feeling settled over me, and I blurted out, "My medicine!"

Bryce turned around. "What about it?"

"I forgot to take it. Last night and this morning."

Sam banged the steering wheel. "I should have reminded you. Where is it?"

"Back at the cabin," I said.

CHAPTER 45

BRYCE

Ashley looked pale, and the memories flooded back of the night years before when Dad found her in my closet, staring at the ceiling, her eyes fixed on something none of us could see. She had thrown up by her bed and wandered into my room and just stood there like a zombie.

I remembered the ambulance and lots of crying and months of trying to forget that awful night. Before her EEGs—brain tests, they told me—she got to stay up late with Dad watching movies so she would sleep once she got to the doctor's office. I was actually jealous of that part, but there was no way I wanted her problem and no way I could take the big pills she did.

They called what she had "complex partial seizures," something about what happens in her brain while she sleeps. The doctor said it was like a computer giving wrong commands. He was trying to stop the bad stuff before her brain got used to it and it started happening while she was awake. Looking at her you wouldn't know anything was wrong, but if she didn't take her medicine, she could get the seizures again.

"Can you hang on, Ashley?" Sam said.

When she didn't answer I turned again to look at her. Her lips trembled, and she was paler than ever. "You okay, Ash?"

"I don't think so," she whispered, her gaze darting around.

This was worse than being chased. And way worse than Boo Heckler. "Sam," I said, "she needs that medicine."

He flew around another curve, craning his neck and looking for something. He hit the brakes and swerved onto an old road that went straight up a hill. He turned left and crashed through some scrub oak at the side of the road. The SUV came to a rest and we all sat, listening. We couldn't see the road from here, but when he rolled down his window, we heard the truck pass.

I gave Sam a thumbs-up, and he backed out of the oaks. I thought we were going to get stuck, but the four-wheel drive took over and we zipped out and back onto the road. We headed back the way we had come.

"We'll get Ashley's medicine, then go to the police station," Sam said. He glanced in his rearview mirror. "Try 911 again."

Ashley shakily handed me the phone and I dialed, but it was dead. Still, I was feeling a lot better about our chances.

My head jerked back as something slammed us from behind.

Ashley screamed and Dylan burst into tears. Sam fought to keep control of the Land Cruiser.

I whirled around. The green car was on our tail.

"Seat belts tight!" Sam said.

CHAPTER 46

ASHLEY

I fought to stay focused. There was no way I could afford a sei-zure now. Bryce said the green car was behind us, but I forced myself not to glance back. It was like monsters in your closet or under your bed—you knew they were in there but you didn't want to look. The car nudged us again, and Sam fought the steering wheel.

I was crying and trying to comfort Dylan at the same time. "If I'd just taken my medicine!" I wailed.

"Stop it," Sam said. "This is not your fault."

Bryce dialed the cell phone again, but it still wasn't working.

Dylan pointed to the left, and I saw a flash of green. The car was right next to us!

It veered right, but Sam swerved and avoided it, jerking our heads to the left. Dylan was crying, and I forced myself to worry about him to get my mind off myself. If only I could distract myself until I got my medicine . . .

The lake was on our right, the reservoir rimmed with a fresh patch of snow. We crossed a bridge and the car kept up, trying to run us into the guardrail. Sam kept both hands on the wheel as the green car pulled just ahead. Sam was going fast—too fast.

Bryce's neck was rigid. He sat ramrod straight, holding on to the grip above his door. Dylan held my arm and whimpered. Air rushed into the SUV as loud as a freight train. It was so cold I could hardly feel my fingers.

"Shh," I whispered to Dylan, "it's going to be all right." But I had spoken too soon.

The green car forced Sam off the road and into a patch of snowy grass where he lost control. We went up an embankment. Sam slammed on the brakes, but it was too late. At the top of the small hill we went airborne, and it felt like the whole world had slipped from beneath us.

Everything went in slow motion. I saw crystal blue water below. Sam's knuckles turned white around the steering wheel. Bryce put both hands on the grip above his door. Dylan's eyes grew wide, and his mouth opened in a silent scream.

Amazing what pops into your head when you think you might die. Would I ever get to talk to Hayley again? Would this be a story we would share? Would the police know this wasn't an accident? Would Mom ever know the truth? Was this what Dad felt like as his plane was going down?

The green car slid to a stop on the road. Our Land Cruiser dipped forward into its freefall toward the water.

A white bird flew by us, its wings flapping lazily, as if nothing in the world was wrong.

Oh, God! I prayed.

CHAPTER 47

BRYCE

I couldn't believe this was happening.

Twice before in my life I thought I was going to die. Once was when I was riding bikes back in Illinois with my friend Tim. We were crossing a road in town, and I looked both ways, but Tim was blocking my view and I didn't see a car coming. I was halfway into the street when the car slammed on its brakes and squealed to a stop.

The driver was just as shaken as I was. "Son, I don't know how I stopped. Must've been some angels looking out for you."

The other time was at my uncle's house in Indiana. While Ashley and I were fooling around with a tractor, she got on and pretended to start it. Only it did start and it raced straight at me. Ashley banged into the back of a hay wagon. If I hadn't jumped out of the way, I would have been flat as a Frisbee.

But neither of us had faced anything like this. As we floated in the air, I thought about my friends and wondered what they would think when they heard that Ashley and I were dead.

The SUV hit the water and the air bags blew into our faces. Like lightning, Sam unfastened his seat belt and tried to open his door, but the water kept it shut. It gushed through the broken window as we sank.

I held my breath as the water rushed in.

Ashley screamed, which made Dylan scream.

Sam yelled, "Don't panic! I'm going to get us out of this."

Ashley stopped screaming, but none of us could calm Dylan.

CHAPTER 48

ASHLEY

Sam helped Bryce out of his seat belt and told Dylan to hold his breath as the water poured over us. "Buddy, we're getting out of here. I promise," he shouted over the torrent.

He fumbled with the car seat, his hands shaking in the freezing water. "We'll go out the broken window. Bryce first, then you, Ashley. I'll follow with Dylan. Swim like crazy to the surface and get to the shore."

We were out of our belts as the freezing water almost filled the Land Cruiser. We floated to the ceiling, where there were a couple of inches of air. The SUV turned slowly, like a boat listing to one side.

"Act fast and don't be afraid," Sam said. "God's going to help you."

I wondered how he knew that.

"Jesus, help us get out of here!" I prayed.

"God, please help us," Bryce said.

Sam held Dylan tight to his chest while the Land Cruiser went fully under. He signaled wildly and pushed Bryce and me toward the open window.

Dylan was holding his breath, but his little face looked chalky and his eyes were glassy. This was a kid who only went into a pool if he had his plastic turtle that held him way above the water.

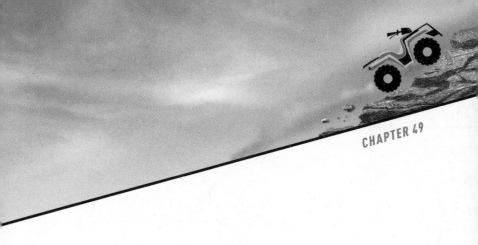

CHAPTER 49

BRYCE

I sucked in a last good lungful of air and dived out the window. The cold water stung my eyes. I turned and reached for Ashley's hand, and she shot out, bubbles streaming from her mouth and nose.

It felt like we had dived into a pitcher of freezing lemonade. The murky water enveloped us and seemed to reach into our souls, trying to take our air away.

We rose hand in hand, struggling to keep from sucking water into our lungs. Just as I thought I couldn't hold my breath any longer, golden rays shimmered above us and we broke to the surface, gasping.

CHAPTER 50

ASHLEY

As soon as Bryce and I reached the surface, I thrashed about, freezing but searching desperately for Dylan and Sam. "They're not going to make it, Bryce!" I screamed. "Dylan will never hold his breath that long!"

Bryce tugged me a few yards to some rocks where we sat huddled, trying to protect each other from the icy wind that froze the water to our clothes and skin. "Please, Jesus, please, Jesus, please, Jesus," was all I could say.

My whole body was numb, even worse than at Dad's funeral,

and I couldn't move my fingers. The frigid water lapped in a lazy rhythm against the rocks.

"I'm going back down," Bryce said.

"No!" I said, holding him with all my might. "Don't try and be a hero. I can't lose you too."

Bryce's lips were blue and quivering, and his eyes were red. "I'm not trying to be a hero. I just want my little brother and my dad to be okay."

His dad? Bryce had never called Sam that before.

I kept my eyes peeled on the water. Dylan could be a pain, but I loved him with all my heart and couldn't imagine life without him. I cried, thinking of how I had yelled at him so many times, but now all I wanted to see was that big head of his coming out of the water. I promised a million things—that I would never complain about his messing up my room or tracking mud in the house after I had just vacuumed or his crying to get his way around Mom.

CHAPTER 51

BRYCE

Ashley and I held each other, shivering and crying and praying. It wasn't praying like you hear at church. It was just us two
begging God for help.

It seemed like years went by, and we didn't see any sign of Dylan
or Sam. I knew Sam would never leave my little brother down there,
and soon I was sure they were both gone. How in the world would
we tell Mom?

Losing one dad is bad enough, I prayed. *Isn't it, God?*

Ashley turned to me and pointed at bubbles rising 10 or 15 feet
from the rock. First it was only a few little bubbles, then a bunch,
then bigger bubbles.

Dylan's head popped through, and Sam held him out toward us. Sam coughed and sputtered as Ashley and I whooped and hollered.

But something was wrong. Dylan wasn't coughing. His face was white, and his eyelids were blue. He looked as limp as a rag doll.

"Take him!" Sam yelled. "Help me get him out!"

We got our hands under Dylan's armpits, but he felt like a sack of potatoes in his water-soaked clothes. Ashley helped me pull him up onto the cold rock.

Sam crawled up quickly, panting. He knelt beside Dylan, but I could tell by the way my little brother's body lay still that he was gone.

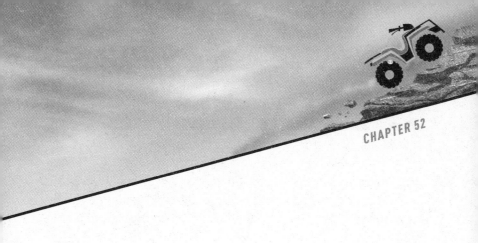

CHAPTER 52

ASHLEY

When Sam rolled Dylan onto his side, Bryce looked shocked too. I could only imagine what those last few seconds in the SUV were like for Sam and Dylan.

Sam's face was all screwed up in a mix of anger and tears while he patted Dylan's back. "Not again," he said through clenched teeth. "You're not putting me through this again."

At first I thought he was talking to Dylan, but then I realized he was praying. I'd never heard him talk to God.

"Breathe!" Sam's voice echoed off the walls of the mountains as he pushed on Dylan's chest. "Make him breathe!"

Then came the sweetest sound I have ever heard. Dylan coughed and burped. Water gurgled from his mouth, and his eyelids fluttered. It was better than Christmas morning.

Sam hugged Dylan to his chest, and Bryce and I sat beside them and put our arms around them. I didn't care that I was freezing or that there were goons out there who wanted to hurt us. My little brother was back, and I saw how much Sam cared about us. We all sat there crying, even Sam, which scared Dylan even more and he began to sob loudly. That made us laugh, which seemed to puzzle him to no end.

All of us were trembling uncontrollably now, and I knew we had to get dry and warm fast or we'd be in trouble.

PART 3

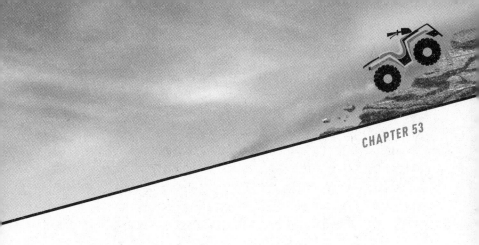

CHAPTER 53

BRYCE

Something special was happening on the rock in that reservoir—something unexplainable. Was God watching us? I'm sure. Were angels protecting us? I think so.

A guy in a Jeep saw us waving and stopped. We scrambled off the rock and piled into his SUV. I held Dylan, trying to warm him, and Sam hugged Ashley. After the driver turned on the heat full blast, Sam told him what had happened. The man drove us to the sheriff's office and stayed with us to make sure we were okay.

They laid out our wet clothes on an old heater and wrapped us in blankets. One of the officers made us hot chocolate while Sam drank coffee. The guy in the Jeep went home and brought back clothes for Sam and robes for Ashley, Dylan, and me. I couldn't help smiling every time I looked at Dylan getting lost in that old robe.

Sam gave the officers the license plate number of the green car, which amazed me. Despite all we had been through, he had memorized it. He also gave them the memory stick he had shoved in his pocket, but it was full of water and I doubted it would work.

"I can't believe those guys wanted to kill us," Ashley said when the officers left us alone.

"Maybe they just wanted to scare us," Sam said.

"They did a good job," I said.

After Sam called Mom, the officers drove us to a nearby hospital to get checked out. It was fun riding in the cruiser, and I expected Dylan to be all over the car. But he just sat next to Sam and held his hand.

A nurse clucked her tongue and said, "You poor things," then led us into a room to wait for the doctor.

The doctor came in and looked at Dylan's eyes with his light. He checked his ears and lungs, then looked the rest of us over and shook his head. "You guys are either very lucky or you have some-body upstairs looking out for you."

CHAPTER 54

ASHLEY

When Mom got to the hospital, Bryce and I ran into her arms.
The only time I've cried harder was the night of the plane crash. She
and Sam hugged a long time too.

Mom's mouth popped open with each new wrinkle in the story.
She put her hand on Sam's arm. "They think it was the people who
stole the gold?"

"Had to be," Sam said.

The real miracle was that I had not had a seizure, even with all
we had been through. The doctor found some medicine and gave it
to me.

A police officer came in and asked Sam to sign a couple of things. "Oh, and the local paper wants to talk with you and take your picture," the officer said.

Sam looked at Mom kind of funny and asked to speak with the officer outside. I was trying to think of what I would say to the reporter when Sam came back and told us we wouldn't be doing any interview or pictures.

"Why not?" Bryce said, looking disappointed.

Sam sighed. "We've had enough excitement for one day."

I don't remember much of the drive home except waking up once and hearing Dylan snore. Bryce slept against the other door. The dashboard lights lit Mom's face, and I saw her wipe away tears as she and Sam listened to the radio. I usually gag when she turns on the Christian station with the slow music, but tonight it felt good to hear those old songs.

Sam carried me to bed when we got home, and it felt so good to be held in his strong arms that I pretended to still be asleep. I knew it wouldn't be long before I started calling him Dad too.

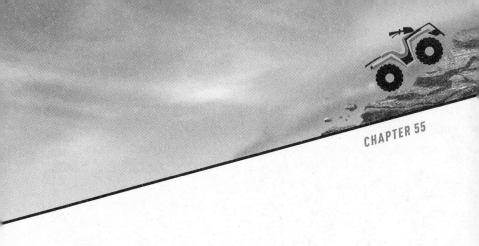

CHAPTER 55

BRYCE

I got up late Sunday, even though I had wanted to go to church and tell all my friends everything that had happened. I could see Ashley and me standing with the pastor, telling our story, thanking God for saving us. Maybe next week.

Leigh seemed amazed at all we'd been through. I was glad Sam had been with us, because I don't think she would have believed it otherwise. She usually treats us as nuisances, but that day she kept smiling at us and playing games with Dylan, which she never does. I wondered how long that would last.

I was feeling better until I noticed our ATVs in their stalls in the barn. We'd cheated death, but I still had to face Boo Heckler the next day.

Sam and Mom subscribe to two newspapers—*The Denver Post* and *The Gazette* from Colorado Springs. Neither carried anything about us, but the report about the stolen gold was on the front page of each. The story said police were following several leads.

I wondered why Sam hadn't wanted our pictures in the papers. Did he really think it was too much for us? Or was he afraid the guys would find out where we lived and come for us? Something about it didn't make sense. I kept looking at Sam, waiting for an explanation, but he seemed different somehow, like something was going on that none of us could understand.

It was cloudy all day, and Ashley and I didn't feel like doing much outside, so we stayed inside. I creamed her playing video games. Then she chose Boggle, Scrabble, and Battleship and beat me at all three.

Dylan cried for his miner's hat, monkey, and raccoon, and Sam promised he would get them back. The police called in the afternoon and said they had pulled the Land Cruiser from the reservoir and that it was totaled—ruined.

Sam fixed dinner that night, and when we all came to the table, Mom had us hold hands. She asked who wanted to say grace.

"Dear God," I prayed, "thanks for getting us out of the water and helping us the way you did. And thank you that Sam was there. Help the police catch those guys so they can't hurt anybody else. Help them find the gold." I took a breath. "And thanks for giving us this food and for making us a family."

Mom squeezed my hand.

Sam coughed and went back to the kitchen.

CHAPTER 56

ASHLEY

I was helping Mom with the dishes when the phone rang. I had wanted to call Hayley and some of my other friends to tell them what had happened, but Mom asked me not to tell them yet.

Sam got the phone, snapped his fingers, and motioned all of us over. He hit the Speakerphone button and said, "Go ahead, sir."

"I thought you'd like to know we caught the guy who ran you off the road," the officer said. "We have him in custody so he's not going to bother you anymore."

The officer told us the man was Gavin Winkler, and they had caught him at the airport in Denver. "He was on his way to Las Vegas." The officer said he hadn't confessed to anything, and they hadn't retrieved the nugget, but there were big scrapes on the right side of his rental car that matched the paint on Sam's SUV. He also said they were going to try and charge him with attempted murder. They weren't sure who had been driving the pickup.

I wondered if they'd catch the second man. Who was the guy with his back turned in the picture? And where was the gold?

That night I lit my candle and started a new diary. I didn't want to wait to get my old one from the cabin. I remembered the situation with Hayley and felt guilty again.

Someone knocked lightly on my door.

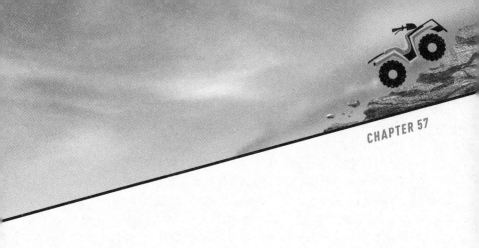

CHAPTER 57

BRYCE

I helped Dylan get ready for bed, then read him his favorite book. Sam tucked him in and said good night, and Dylan kissed his cheek. I didn't remember that happening before.

Sam followed me to my room and sat on my bed as I got under the covers. He sat there a long time, just looking at me. "I was proud of you in the SUV, Bryce," he said finally. "You kept your head."

"None of us would have gotten out if it hadn't been for you," I said. I felt the corners of my mouth giving way like a riverbank about to fall into the rushing water.

Sam looked at the floor and put his hands together. "A lot of adults wouldn't have been able to do what you and Ashley did."

"Thanks," I said. It seemed like Sam wanted to say more, but maybe he couldn't find the words.

He scratched at an eye and leaned back. "About tomorrow. I know this Boo kid is on your tail and could cause problems."

I nodded and sighed.

"I have a trip planned in the morning, but I could get another pilot to take my place. With all that's happened, it might be good. Plus, if you needed a little backup, I could be here."

Sam was doing what my dad would have done. Dad used to sit on my bed, talking about stuff before I went to sleep. He never seemed too busy. Sam seemed a little nervous, but at least he was trying.

"Don't cancel your trip," I said. "I have to face Boo sooner or later by myself. I'm scared, but I'll be okay."

He patted my shoulder. "One more thing. Keep this weekend to yourself for a couple of days. It'll be hard not telling your friends, but your mom and I think it's best."

"I can't tell anybody?"

There was something he wasn't telling me. "Trust me," he said, "like you trusted me in the SUV."

I fell asleep imagining the school might have a special assembly where Ashley and I told our stories. We would be bold and not hold back about the way God had kept us calm, and kids would flock to the front and ask us where we went to church. Boo might ask for my autograph instead of pounding me into the pavement.

How could I keep quiet about something like this?

CHAPTER 58

ASHLEY

It was Mom at my door. I closed my diary and told her the whole story of what had happened at Hayley's house. I could tell she was shocked, and I expected her to shake her head and say she was disappointed in me or that I could never go back to Hayley's again. But she just hugged me a long time.

"I'm glad you told me," she said. "It must have been hard holding it in."

I nodded. Then the tears came. "I'm sorry, Mom. I let you down and I disappointed God, and Hayley must think I'm a hypocrite."

"You might be surprised. Just tell her how you feel. She might hear you."

"But I want her to believe so bad," I said.

Mom scooted closer. "You don't have to be perfect to help somebody know God. What attracts people most is when you're honest and real and don't try to be someone you're not."

"I guess so. Like Pastor Jackson. He doesn't just tell us about when he does good things. He tells us when he blows it."

"Exactly."

"I guess I thought you were supposed to do everything right, and if you didn't God was mad at you."

Mom smiled. "God's not mad at you. I'm sure he was sad about you seeing the stuff in that movie, because he knew it would hurt you. But God doesn't pull his love away if you do something wrong. He loves you all the way."

"But doesn't he correct us?"

"Yes, but not because he's mad at you. He's like the father in the parable about the Prodigal Son. He's standing at the window, watching and waiting for you to come back, ready to sweep you up in his arms."

I asked what she thought I should tell Hayley the next day.

"Why not invite her over after school? You two can talk and do your homework here."

"But what do I say?"

She kissed me on the forehead. "Tell her the truth. And let God do the rest."

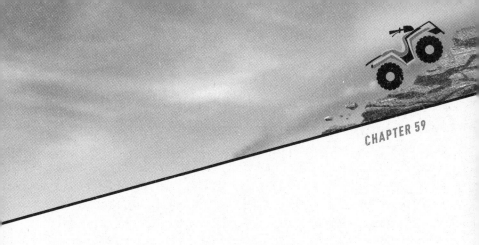

CHAPTER 59

BRYCE

I kept dreaming about Boo and what he was going to do when he caught me at school. I was purple all over and had blood on every shirt I owned. Then I dreamed of going underwater in Sam's Land Cruiser. I had a feeling I was going to relive that for a long time.

When I woke up and looked at the clock, I bolted from my bed and went downstairs for breakfast. Ashley had already finished and was in the shower. Mom had a bowl set out for my cereal. I'm a cereal mixer—I won't eat any cereal that's not mixed with at least two others. This morning I chose Honey Nut Cheerios, Corn Flakes, and Frosted Mini-Wheats.

Mom put the Denver paper in front of me and pointed to a picture. It was the guy in the Cincinnati Reds hat being put in a police cruiser. Gavin Winkler. On the other side of the page was a picture of our SUV being hauled out of the reservoir. The back end was smashed, and you could see mud on the license plate.

The story said Winkler had forced a Land Cruiser off the road as he fled and that a man and his three children had survived the crash. I skipped to the end where it said the gold hadn't been recovered.

I kept looking for our names, but they weren't there. I wanted the story to say that Winkler was trying to hurt us and broke into our cabin and was afraid of the picture we had taken of him. But now I couldn't even tell my friends what had happened. It wasn't fair.

After a quick shower, I grabbed my backpack and hoped I looked okay. When my hair gets a little longer it doesn't cooperate. Duncan Swift says when it sticks up in the back I look like a chicken.

Sam had gassed up our ATVs, and they were sitting outside the barn. He waved as Ashley and I rode through the field by our house toward the school. It feels good to ride when you have a lot on your mind. The hum of the engine and concentrating on not hitting ruts and rocks can soothe you.

We followed the road to our left all the way to a golf course entrance, where we crossed a small bridge and went through another field. When we approached Mrs. Watson's farm, someone was standing on the hill where I'd last seen Boo.

CHAPTER 60

ASHLEY

Bryce and I waved at Mrs. Watson and headed for school the long way, skirting the hill and going through the gymnasium entrance. Bryce kept looking back as we walked inside and found our lockers. Over the weekend the administration had installed a new litter of cardboard cats in the hallways. These all had smiles like the Cheshire cat in *Alice in Wonderland.*

Down the hall a custodian had a ladder against the wall and was taking down a stuffed cat that had been strung by a coat hanger from one of the ceiling tiles. The cat had the face of our football coach pasted on it, and a bunch of kids stood around snickering.

Instead of going to our regular first period, they were giving the test in our homeroom. Bryce went on to class, and I put some things in my locker. When I closed the door, I saw Hayley standing there.

"Hey," I said, "I was going to invite you to my house tonight."

She frowned. "Can't. My mom found out about us watching that movie. My sister ratted us out."

"You're in trouble?"

She nodded. "If you could tell my mom it was your idea, that would really help. She doesn't want me having you over anymore because you came when they weren't there—"

"She didn't know I was coming?" I said. "But you said she would be there."

"I kind of forgot. So can you tell her it was your idea?"

"Let's talk about it at lunch," I said.

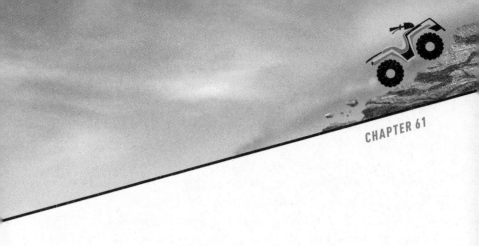

CHAPTER 61

BRYCE

I said hi to Duncan and Skeeter before I got ready for the first CAT. It killed me not to tell them what had happened. It was like winning a million dollars on a TV show and not being able to tell anyone.

Ashley came in looking like someone had punched her in the stomach. I wanted to ask what was wrong, but the teacher came in and turned on the television. The test was coordinated with every other class in the state.

A picture of a big white cat came on the screen, and somebody groaned. We were sick of cats. Even people who liked cats were sick of cats. I thought I was getting a hair ball. We just wanted the tests over.

I found only one short pencil with the lead worn to a nub. I glanced at Ashley, pointed to my pencil, and she went through her backpack and pulled out a new one for me. The teacher glared at us like we had defiled the sacred CAT process. Every teacher made a big deal about us having two sharpened pencils, and I felt like a CAT traitor.

At exactly one minute after the hour, the color bars on the screen went black and a nicely dressed woman appeared, sitting on the front of her desk, a real cat on her lap.

"Welcome to this year's most exciting educational event in the state of Colorado," she purred, flashing pearly white teeth. Did she have cat whiskers painted on her face? "Over the next five days we are going to probe your minds and find out if we're doing our jobs as educators. So in a sense, this test is not about you—it's about your teachers. Please sit back, relax, and enjoy these next five days."

In the middle of her talk about the test (which included a long section about not cheating), the cat walked behind her and started pawing at an apple. It knocked the apple to the floor, then jumped down after it.

The whole class roared. Our teacher touched a finger to his lips, but I imagined every seventh grade class in the state laughing.

The first part of the test was reading comprehension. We had to pick out the main point of the story, retell the story, and write an essay about the main character to show we could actually read and understand the words, I guess. I understood most of it, but some I had to read over two or three times. I looked forward to the math section. I felt more comfortable with numbers than stories.

Once I looked out the window at a pond in a pasture and thought of being underwater. I couldn't believe I was sitting at my desk taking a test when they could have been planning my funeral.

And I couldn't tell anybody!

CHAPTER 62

ASHLEY

Twice a week Mom lets us buy our lunch, and that day I
grabbed some pizza and found a seat in the back. I asked God to help
me say the right things to Hayley. When I looked up, she was coming toward me.

After we talked about the tests, I pushed my plate away and leaned
toward her. "Listen, I need to talk to you about the other night."

"I shouldn't have asked you to tell my mom it was your idea,"
she said.

"The thing is, I'm a Christian, and I should have said something
about the movie and not watched it."

Hayley took her sandwich apart, then put it back together. "I know you're a Christian. What's that got to do with anything?"

"I should have said something, but I was scared you'd think I was a goody-goody. I've felt bad about the whole thing for days. The truth is, if I'd have said something, you might not be in trouble."

She looked at me with a glint in her eyes. "Yeah, it was your fault." She smiled. "You know, I'm a Christian too."

"Really?"

"Yeah, we go to church and stuff. Not very often, but I believe in Jesus and all that."

I'd heard this kind of thing before, and every time it reminds me of myself. I once thought I was a Christian because I went to church at Christmas and Easter and believed Jesus was a real person. But it didn't actually change anything until I understood what the Bible really taught and I saw how much God loved me.

"Maybe we should get together and do a Bible study or something," I said. "Would your mom allow that?"

"I don't know. . . ."

"It's worth a try, don't you think?"

I was dying to tell Hayley what had happened to us over the weekend. The way Mom and Sam were treating this seemed strange, but then nobody had ever tried to kill us before either.

CHAPTER 63

BRYCE

I ate lunch in a corner of the hallway where I thought nobody would see me. Skeeter, who has always had a thing for Ashley, finally came up and asked why I was hiding. I shrugged.

He rolled his eyes. "I get it. Boo's still after you."

"Keep it down," I said, glancing down the hall.

"There's no hiding," Skeeter said. "He's going to get you one way or another. And if he wants those four-wheelers of yours, he'll get them."

"No way," I said. "If you don't stand up to somebody like Boo, he'll walk over you your whole life."

"I'd rather be walked over than dead." He leaned forward. "Plus, I'm scared that you and Ashley are going to get hurt."

I wanted to tell Skeeter about the reservoir. I heard people talk about the stolen gold and could hardly hold my tongue.

When the tests were over for the day, I went to gym class and changed in the locker room.

The gym teacher, Mr. Baldwin, had set up an obstacle course, and we spent the period clocking our best speeds around hurdles, rings, and obstructions. We had to crawl through one enclosed area, run down the balance beam (which nobody could do), do push-ups and chin-ups, make a layup, jump the pommel horse, and run a lap around the gym.

In every class I've ever been in, there's always one kid who is the biggest and clumsiest. At Red Rock Middle School, that guy is Chuck Burly. He's the funniest kid in school, but he's also the fattest. His face is always puffy and red, and he kind of hobbles when he walks, like he's carrying a piano. I was cheering for him as he ran through the gym when I saw two people sneak into the boys' locker room. From the back it looked like Boo, who usually wore a jean jacket, but I wasn't sure.

Chuck couldn't clear the hurdles, so he just jumped high enough to knock them over and kept going. He stepped on the balance beam, and I held my breath. Usually people fall right off, but Chuck scooted sideways, and when he hit the floor with a boom at the end of the beam everybody gave it up, clapping for him. He got stuck in the crawling thing, so Mr. Baldwin stopped the timer and moved it wider.

In the end, Chuck had the slowest time of the whole class, but he was the only one who got all the way across the beam without falling.

The bell rang and I slapped his sweaty back. "Sure looked good out there today."

Chuck smiled. "Slow but sure. Give all the credit to my new eating plan. It's called the seafood diet."

"The seafood diet?"

"Whatever food I see, I eat."

I had the feeling he told those kinds of jokes on himself so no one else would.

Chuck stopped laughing as we entered the locker room. My backpack lay in the middle of the floor, my books strewn around the place. One sock hung from a fluorescent light and another floated in the toilet. My pants were tied in several knots. Tight. Boo couldn't have done this without help.

Coach Baldwin came in and looked the place over. "Timberline, in my office. Now."

CHAPTER 64

ASHLEY

I was heading to my next-to-last class, wondering what Mom would say about my talk with Hayley, when someone blocked my path. Somebody big. At first I thought it was a teacher, but when I saw the dirty jean jacket, I knew.

"Hey, Timber girl," Boo said with a sneer. "Tell your brother I'll be waiting for him outside after school. I saw you drove your precious little four-wheelers today, right?"

I figured it was none of his business, so I said nothing. I didn't even nod. I don't like anyone making fun of my last name—certainly not Boo.

"Left him a little reminder in gym, but don't forget to tell him—"
Boo leaned down, and I could smell cheeseburger on his breath—
"or I'll knock all that metal on your teeth down your throat."

I let Boo pass. I'd learned that ignoring a bully was one of the
best ways not to let him or her get to you. But this was a little hard
to ignore.

Especially the part about knocking the metal down my throat.

CHAPTER 65

BRYCE

"Who did it?" Coach Baldwin said. Baldwin was a good name for him because his head looked like a lightbulb with hair on the side. He was thin, stood about six feet tall, and had chest and abdominal muscles that reminded people of professional wrestlers.

"D-did what, sir?" I said.

He cocked his head. "You threw your own socks in the toilet and tied your pants in knots?"

I shook my head.

"Who did it?"

I told him who I thought might have.

Coach shook his head. "Need some help with Heckler?"

"I th-think I have it under c-control," I said.

Coach smiled. "At least let me help you untie your pants."

I was late to my last class, but Coach Baldwin wrote me a note. While Mrs. Ferguson went to the office and left us working on an essay, Ashley told me what Boo had said to her in the hall. That made me mad. Until now he hadn't said much to her, but this changed things.

"Why don't we tell the principal or Coach Baldwin about Boo's e-mail?" Ashley said.

"Boo will just get us some other way," I said. "We need to handle this ourselves."

"Bryce, that's crazy. The guy is twice as big as you. He makes the Hulk look like a weenie."

"Ash, I have to stand up to him."

"Your pride's gonna get us killed."

If I knew karate or had pepper spray or a stun gun it would be different.

My cell phone vibrated. I had a new text message from Sam.

You have what it takes. If you can escape those guys in Gold Town, you can show this Boo character what you're made of.

CHAPTER 66

ASHLEY

I followed Bryce out of our last class with the feeling that Boo and his little friend might jump us any second. We stopped at our lockers and put our stuff away.

No Boo.

The bus kids sprinted outside. Some of the drivers went by their own clock, and if you didn't make it on in time they shut the door. A few of our friends looked at us like we were about to walk the plank.

Outside the Colorado sun beat down. Mom boasted there were more than 300 days of sunshine each year, unlike Chicago where in the winter God threw a gray blanket over the sky and it didn't come off until spring.

"Nice day to get beat up," Bryce's friend Duncan said as he passed.

"Thanks a lot," I said. Duncan is cute and one of the best at sports in our whole class. I'm not sure he knows I exist, except that I'm Bryce's sister.

We walked through the parking lot and over the little rise that led to Mrs. Watson's house. I saw two people in the distance, between us and the barn.

"Wait up," Skeeter called from behind us. He ran over to us, legs and arms swinging wildly.

"Skeeter, this isn't your fight," Bryce said.

He caught his breath and looked at me. "I know. But I didn't want you to think you were all alone."

Bryce patted his shoulder. "Thanks, but we need to do this on our own."

Skeeter glanced at me. "You sure?"

I nodded and he walked back toward the school.

Bryce gripped one strap of his backpack as if trying to keep from falling overboard. "You ready?" he said.

"No."

"Me either."

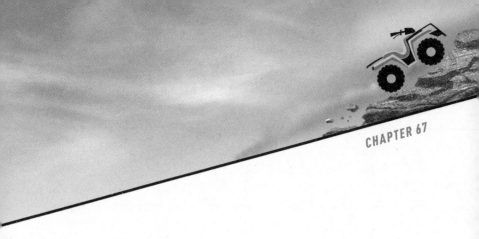

CHAPTER 67

BRYCE

I stopped two yards from Boo and his friend and put my backpack down. Ashley stood behind me.

"So, you gonna let us ride?" the little one said.

I stared at Boo.

"Answer us," he said, sneering and stepping closer. "Or just hand over the keys."

I wondered if Boo had ever really beat anyone up. He scared people and pulled a lot of threatening pranks, but the more I thought about it, maybe he was all show. I couldn't remember when he had actually hit someone.

Who was I kidding? This guy had fists the size of cinder blocks.

"We're not allowed to let anybody ride them," I said, my voice shaky. But I hadn't stuttered. That was a start. "If you have a problem with that, you're talking to the wrong person."

"Hiding behind your daddy?" Boo said. "Where's he now? Huh?"

I held my ground and kept staring.

Ashley stepped forward. "We have your e-mail. Coach Baldwin knows what you did in the locker room. You want to be expelled, keep it up."

"Ooh, I'm so scared," Boo said. He made a fist. "I'll ask you one more time. You gonna let us ride?"

I had always loved the story of David and Goliath, but right now I didn't have a slingshot. "No," I said, and the strength in my voice surprised me. "Leave us alone, Aaron."

Boo slapped me hard.

Ashley gasped and stepped back.

I put a hand to my face, and it was hot. "You *slapped* me?" I said, squinting at him.

He looked flustered and glanced at his friend. Then at me. "Come on, put 'em up."

"You've never actually been in a fight, have you?" I said. "You just intimidate everybody."

I knew my face was red, but inside I was smiling.

A truck raced to the end of the school parking lot and Boo turned.

"I'm still gonna get you," he said. "And we'll have those four-wheelers."

As Boo and his little friend hurried away, Ashley patted me on the shoulder. "You okay?"

"Yeah." I rubbed my face. I knew the verse about turning the other cheek, and I was glad I hadn't had to.

CHAPTER 68

ASHLEY

As we got on the ATVs, Mrs. Watson called out from her door. Bryce took off toward the pasture, and I rode to her house.

"Your uncle was here asking for you," she said. "I told him what time you got out of school, and he said he'd see you when you got home."

Uncle? Our uncle Terry had died, and as far as we knew Sam didn't have a brother. I thanked Mrs. Watson and tried to catch up with Bryce. He was waiting on the knoll near the school. I glanced at the truck in the parking lot and wondered if it had been some kind of coincidence or if Sam had sent someone to protect us. *Our uncle?*

We rode into the pasture. Halfway home, I noticed the truck going slowly on the road beside us. I couldn't see the driver, but the license plate was green and white like the Colorado plates Sam and Mom have.

We were almost to the house when the pickup sped into our driveway, kicking up dust. It zoomed through our yard and came straight at us, stopping a few yards from us. That's when I remembered where I had seen it before.

On Gold Camp Road.

CHAPTER 69

BRYCE

When a man in a ski mask jumped from the driver's side, Ashley and I gunned our engines, went around the truck, and headed for our front door.

The man got back in the truck and followed, but we were off our bikes and on the front porch before he could get out.

We ran inside, the man catching up to us, and before we could close the door, he stuck his foot in it.

Mom appeared, her glasses pushed down on her nose, which meant she had been working on her book. Pippin and Frodo barked from the backyard.

"What in the world?" Mom said as we pushed with all our might to get the door closed. It burst open, pushing us all back, and Ski Mask was inside.

Mom grabbed us and thrust us behind her. "What do you want?"

"The computer," he said, his voice muffled.

"What computer?" my mother yelled. "Get out of our house!"

The man pulled a gun from his belt, waved it toward the living-room couch, and motioned for us to sit.

My cell phone was in my pocket. If I could dial 911 quickly, the guy would never know it.

"The computer with the e-mail," he said. "Now!"

"I don't know what you're talking about!" Mom said.

"They do," the man said. "You sent an e-mail from the cabin before the power was cut. Now where is it?"

I looked at Mom. "Did you open an e-mail from me Friday night?"

"You know I don't check e-mail while I'm writing. It probably downloaded but—"

"Tell me where it is right now, lady, or one of these kids gets hurt."

"In my office."

The man gestured with the gun for us to stand. "Show me."

CHAPTER 70

ASHLEY

I don't know about Bryce, but all I could think was, *This is not why I moved to Colorado!*

I heard a beep as we entered Mom's office.

The man stopped.

Another beep.

"What's that?" he said.

A third beep.

He grabbed Bryce's arm and out came his cell phone. The man snatched it out of his hand and punched the red button, stopping the call. He threw the phone to the floor and pointed at Bryce. "Try that again and you're dead."

Mom's laptop lay on the desk with lots of papers and mail stacked nearby. The man grabbed the laptop, closed it, and unplugged it from its docking station.

"You can't take that," Mom said. "That has all my work on it!"

"Downstairs," he said.

If only I could slip away and call Sam or the police. Something. Anything. But if one of us ran, the man would shoot. Maybe I could distract him.

"How did you find us?" I said.

"Just get downstairs. Sit on the couch."

"You were pretty smart to track us here."

As we sat, the man said, "I've got my ways."

I looked at Bryce. "Now there's no way they'll be able to find out who Winkler's accomplice was. He has the only file of our picture."

"Shut up, missy," the man said.

"And you're the guy with his back to us at Gold Town, talking to Winkler, right? Which means you have the gold."

"Please don't take my computer," Mom said. "All my work is on that hard drive. Do you know how long it took—?"

"Shut up!" the man said, and I thought I recognized his voice.

"Bet you're glad that Winkler guy's been put away," I said. "Now you won't have to share any of the loot."

The man just stared at us. When a siren sounded in the distance, he ran to the window and searched the horizon.

"Guess my 911 call went through," Bryce said. "You should have left the phone on and told them it was a mistake."

"Shut up!"

"You can't say that," a tiny voice said from behind us. It was Dylan, rubbing his eyes. "You're not supposed to say shut up."

"Honey, come here," Mom said, picking Dylan up.

The man's gaze darted around the room, and he scratched the top of his head. He ordered us into the kitchen, herded us into the food pantry, and jammed something against the door to block us in.

We heard footsteps through the kitchen toward the front. The screen slammed. Then someone yelped, and there was a thump.

Seconds passed.

"Hello?" Leigh called. "Anybody home?"

We yelled for her to let us out.

"Who's the guy with the gun?" she said, opening the door.

"Long story," Bryce said. "Where is he?"

CHAPTER 71

BRYCE

I tore through the living room ahead of Mom and Ashley, only to find the guy with the mask on the ground in our front yard holding his leg. The laptop lay on the concrete like a wounded animal. The monitor had broken off, and pieces of plastic were scattered all over. The Creep was holding the gun on the man.

"Randy!" I shouted. "What happened?"

"This guy was coming out while we were going in," Randy said. "I must have surprised him, because he turned and tripped over that snow shovel. The gun flew out of his hand. What was he doing?"

"Trying to destroy the evidence," Ashley said, gathering up Mom's laptop.

There was no siren now, so the 911 call must not have gone through. Mom called the police.

A few minutes later an officer cuffed the man, then pulled his mask off. He had a patchy mustache and dark hair.

Ashley gasped. "The deputy! You came to our cabin!"

The man cursed us as he was led to the squad car.

We explained what had happened at the cabin.

The officer said he had read about it. "You saying this guy might be the one with the gold?"

"Could be why he came here," Ashley said. "We have a picture of him talking with Winkler, but he had his back turned to the camera. We didn't even know we had it."

"Uh, actually we didn't have it," I said. I had hooked the laptop to a monitor and was looking over Mom's e-mail files. "I guess it never came through."

"He came here to destroy a file that didn't exist?" the officer said. "Real sharp."

Leigh was peering into the man's truck. "There's a suitcase behind the seat." She tried to lift it, but it was too heavy. Randy pulled it out with a grunt and put it on the ground.

The guy in the squad car kicked the back of the seat and hollered.

Randy clicked the latch and opened it. "Holy gold mine!"

The nugget was still in its glass case, and when the sun hit it, the thing sparkled like a mountain stream.

The officer pushed his hat back on his head and chuckled.

Dylan ran and stuck his head inside the suitcase. "Can I hold the shiny rock?"

CHAPTER 72

ASHLEY

Sam was as surprised as we were about the deputy. When Bryce told him the man had been in our house with a gun, Sam's face fell. But then he said he was glad that Bryce hadn't moved the snow shovel.

Mom was relieved her book was safe, and from then on she began e-mailing it to herself and printing each chapter after she finished. She called Hayley's mom and explained what had happened between us and asked if we could try to be friends again. Hayley was allowed to come to our house, but only if Mom was home.

Bryce and I decided not to call Randy The Creep anymore. It was the least we could do. Bryce was wary of Boo for the rest of the week, but the bully left us alone. Coach Baldwin had him scrubbing bathrooms during gym class. I guess it helps to have friends in high places.

One afternoon the sheriff came and apologized for all that had happened. He explained that the deputy and Winkler had worked with the store owner to steal the gold. The boy at the store turned out to be the owner's son, and he had told his father about giving the memory stick to Bryce.

"When the exhibit opens again, we'd like to have you up to see it," the sheriff said. He handed Sam the miner's hat and a soggy monkey and raccoon.

"We'd like that," Sam said.

The sheriff mentioned the reward, but Sam took him outside to talk.

We kept watching for a newspaper story of the gold heist to tell who had cracked the case. Finally, *The Gazette* linked the deputy with Winkler and the shop owner and exposed their plan. The report never mentioned that a 13-year-old taking a picture threw a wrench in the heist.

Dylan kept asking Sam if he could go back and play on the "Ping-Pong machine." Sam promised we'd return as soon as the cabin owner let us, which probably wouldn't happen since the place was trashed.

Even with the case solved and the bad guys in jail, Sam seemed upset. I wondered if it was because we were almost killed in the SUV or if he blamed himself for not being home when the deputy forced his way into our house. Or was God working on him?

When we got home from church Sunday, Sam spoke with Mom alone in their room.

Mom was crying when she came out. "Get your brother and meet us in the living room."

CHAPTER 73

BRYCE

Ashley seemed as curious as me. Leigh sat on the couch. She'd been taking a nap and had bad pillow hair and a crease across her face. They let Dylan play out back on the swing set—that's how serious the meeting was.

Mom was still wiping away tears when Sam sat on the hearth in front of the empty fireplace, put his elbows on his knees, and rubbed his hands together.

I was getting nervous. "What's going on?"

Sam and Mom looked at each other, and one of those moments passed between them—the kind that let you know they had talked about something. She dipped her head and her chin quivered. Sam looked at the floor.

I was afraid it had something to do with us. Were they going to split up? I couldn't imagine that. Did they need to sell our ATVs? Had Ashley's disease gotten worse?

Just when I thought I couldn't take it anymore, Sam spoke. "Your mom has known this for some time, but I hadn't told her everything. Until now. I don't know how to say this really. . . ."

"Just say it, Dad," Leigh said.

He nodded. "I'm sorry you haven't been able to talk about this either, Leigh. But talking would endanger us all."

"What do you mean?" Ashley said.

Sam looked at us through tears. "I'm so sorry. You have to believe me."

Ashley started to cry. "What are you sorry for?"

"For killing your father."

ABOUT THE AUTHORS

JERRY B. JENKINS is the author of more than 195 books, including the best-selling Left Behind series—which was named among America's 100 favorite novels by PBS in their Great American Read series. His books have sold more than 71 million copies, including 21 *New York Times* bestsellers. Jerry was inducted into the Colorado Authors' Hall of Fame in 2019. His writing has appeared in *Time*, *Reader's Digest*, *Parade*, *Guideposts*, *Christianity Today*, and dozens of other periodicals, and he was featured on the cover of *Newsweek* magazine in 2004. Jerry teaches nearly 2,000 students online through his Jerry Jenkins Writers Guild. He blogs about writing at JerryJenkins.com.

Jerry has been awarded five honorary doctorates. He and his wife, Dianna, have three grown sons and eight grandchildren.

CHRIS FABRY is an award-winning author and radio personality who hosts the daily program *Chris Fabry Live* on Moody Radio. He is also heard on *Love Worth Finding*, *Building Relationships with Dr. Gary Chapman*, and other radio programs. A 1982 graduate of the W. Page Pitt School of Journalism at Marshall University and a native of West Virginia, Chris and his wife, Andrea, now live in Arizona and are the parents of nine children.

Chris's novels have won five Christy Awards, an ECPA Christian Book Award, and two Awards of Merit from *Christianity Today*. He was inducted into the Christy Award Hall of Fame in 2018. His books include movie novelizations, like the bestseller *War Room*; nonfiction; and novels for children and young adults. He coauthored the Left Behind: The Kids series with Jerry B. Jenkins and Tim LaHaye, as well as the Red Rock Mysteries and the Wormling series with Jerry B. Jenkins. Visit his website at chrisfabry.com.

The Wormling

A thrilling, action-packed fantasy from the minds of Jerry B. Jenkins and Chris Fabry that pits ultimate evil against ultimate good.

Book I
The Book of the King

Book II
The Sword of the Wormling

Book III
The Changeling

Book IV
The Minions of Time

Book V
The Author's Blood

FOR ADVENTURERS

The Wormling series

Red Rock Mysteries series

FOR COMEDIANS

The Dead Sea Squirrels series

FOR ARTISTS

Made to Create with All My
Heart and Soul

Be Bold

FOR ANIMAL LOVERS

Winnie the Horse Gentler series

Starlight Animal Rescue series

CP1337